HOME *on the* RANCH

HOME *on the* RANCH

IN A COWBOY'S ARMS

—— ✗ ——

REBECCA WINTERS

◆ **HARLEQUIN**® HOME ON THE RANCH

Recycling programs
for this product may
not exist in your area.

ISBN-13: 978-1-335-45338-9

In a Cowboy's Arms

Copyright © 2014 by Rebecca Winters

Printed in U.S.A.

™ www.Harlequin.com

Rebecca Winters, whose family of four children has now swelled to include five beautiful grandchildren, lives in Salt Lake City, Utah, in the land of the Rocky Mountains. Living near canyons and high alpine meadows full of wildflowers, she never runs out of places to explore. They, plus her favorite vacation spots in Europe, often end up as backgrounds for her romance novels, because writing is her passion, along with her family and church.

Rebecca loves to hear from readers. If you wish to email her, please visit her website, cleanromances.net.

To Dr. Shane Doyle of the Crow Nation in Montana for his assistance with some aspects of the culture you can't find in a book.

Chapter 1

"Zane? I'm glad you called me back!"

Zane Lawson was the brother-in-law of Sadie Corkin's late mother, Eileen, and uncle of Sadie's half brother. The recently retired navy SEAL had just gone through a painful divorce, yet Sadie could always count on him.

"You sound upset," Zane said. "What's wrong?"

She picked up the Vienna sausage two-year-old Ryan had thrown to the floor and put it in the sink. Her half brother, who had clear blue eyes like his mother, thought he was a big boy and didn't like sitting in the high chair, but today she hadn't given him a choice.

"I got a call from the ranch a little while ago. My father died at the hospital in White Lodge earlier this morning."

Quiet followed for a moment while he digested the news. "His liver?"

"Yes."

"I thought he had years left."

"I did, too. But Millie said the way he drank, it was a miracle that diseased organ of his held up this long." Daniel Corkin's alcohol addiction had caught up with him at a young age, but the impact of the news was still catching up to Sadie. It had been eight years since she'd last seen him. She felt numb inside.

"With news like this, you shouldn't be alone. I'll drive right over."

"What would I do without you?"

"That goes both ways. Have you made any plans yet?"

She'd already talked to Mac and Millie Henson, the foreman and housekeeper on the Montana ranch who'd virtually raised Sadie after her parents' bitter divorce.

"We've decided to hold the graveside service at the Corkin family plot on Saturday. That's as far as I've gotten." She had a lot of decisions to make in the next five days. "I'll have to fly there on Friday."

"Rest assured I'll go to Montana with you so I can help take care of Ryan. See you in a couple of minutes."

"Thank you. Just let yourself in," she said before hanging up. No two-year-old could have a more devoted uncle than Zane.

Ryan had never got to meet his father, Tim Lawson. Tim had owned the software store where Sadie had been hired after she'd moved to San Francisco to be with her mother, Eileen, eight years ago.

Sometimes her mom dropped by the store to go to lunch with her and that's how Eileen had met Tim. It must have been fate because the two had fallen in love and married soon after. But Tim had died in a car accident while Sadie's mother was still expecting their baby. Tragically, Eileen had passed away during the delivery from cardiac arrest brought on by arrhythmia. Age and stress had been a factor.

Sadie suffered from the same condition as her mother. In fact, just before she'd left the ranch, she'd been advised to give up barrel racing and had been put on medication. If she ever married, getting pregnant would be a huge consideration no matter the efficacy of today's drugs.

Sadie had continued to work in sales for Tim's store even after new management had taken over. Since Eileen's death, however, and taking on fulltime duties as a mother to Ryan, she worked for the store from home.

Tim's younger brother, Zane, had been a tower of strength, and the two of them had bonded in their grief over Tim and Eileen's deaths.

Zane knew the whole painful history of the Corkin family, starting with Sadie's great-grandfather Peter Corkin from Farfields, England. Due to depressed times in his own country, he'd traveled to Montana in 1920 to raise Herefords on a ranch he'd named after the town he'd left behind. When he'd discovered that Rufus Bannock, a Scot on the neighboring ranch who ran Angus cattle, had found oil, the Corkins' own lust for oil kicked into gear, but nothing had turned up so far.

Sadie's father, Daniel Corkin, had been convinced there was oil to be found somewhere on his eighty-five-acre ranch. His raging obsession and jealousy of the Bannock luck, coupled with his drinking and suspicions about his wife's infidelity, which were totally unfounded, had driven Eileen away. When she'd filed for divorce, he said he'd give her one, but she would have to leave eight-year-old Sadie with him.

Terrified that if she stayed in the marriage he'd kill her as he'd sworn to do, Eileen had given up custody of their daughter, forcing Millie Henson, the Corkin housekeeper, to raise Sadie along with her own child, Liz.

Zane also knew Mac and Millie Henson were saints as far as Sadie was concerned, and she felt she could never repay their goodness and devotion.

It was their love that had sheltered her and seen her through those unhappy childhood years with an angry, inebriated father who'd lost the ability to love. The Hensons had done everything possible to provide a loving family atmosphere, but Sadie had suffered from acute loneliness.

Once, when she was fifteen, there'd been a mother-daughter event at the school. Never really understanding how her mother could have abandoned her, Sadie had been in too much pain to tell Millie about the school function and had taken off on her horse, Candy, not caring where she was going.

Eventually stopping somewhere on the range, Sadie, thinking she was alone, had slumped forward in the saddle, heaving great, uncontrollable sobs. With only her horse to hear, she'd given way to her grief, wondering if she might die of it....

"What's so terrible on a day like this?"

Sadie knew that deep voice. *Jarod Bannock.*

She lifted her head and stared through tear-drenched eyes at the striking, dark-haired eighteen-year-old. She knew two things about Jarod Bannock. One, his mother had been an Apsáalooke Indian. Two, every girl in the county knocked themselves out for his attention. If any of them had succeeded, she didn't know about it—although he was a neighbor, her family never spoke of him. Her father, whose hatred knew no bounds, held an irrational predjudice against Jarod because of his heritage.

"I miss my mother."

Jarod smiled at her, compassion in his eyes.

"When I miss mine, I ride out here, too. This is where the First Maker hovers as he watches his creation. He says, 'If you need to contact me, you will find me along the backbone of the earth where I travel as I guard my possessions.' He knows your sadness, Sadie, and has provided you a horse to be your comfort."

His words sent shivers up her spine. She felt a compelling spirituality in them, different from anything she'd experienced at church with Millie.

"Do you want to see some special horses?" he asked her. "They're hard to find unless you know where to look for them."

"You mean, the feral horses Mac sometimes talks about?"

"Yes. I'll take you to them."

Having lost both parents himself, Jarod understood what was going on inside her better than anyone else. Wordlessly he led her up the canyon, through the twists and turns of rock formations she'd never seen before.

They rode for a good five minutes before he reined to a stop and put a finger to his lips. She pulled back on Candy's reins and waited until she heard the pounding of hooves. Soon a band of six horses streaked through the gulch behind a large, grayish tan stallion with black legs and mane. The power of the animals mesmerized her.

"You see that grullo in the lead? The one with the grayish hairs on his body?"

"Yes," she whispered breathlessly.

"That's his harem."

"What's a harem?"

"The mares he mates with and controls. Keep watching and you'll see some bachelor stallions following them."

Sure enough a band of eight horses came flying through after the first group. "Why aren't they all together?"

"They want control of Chief's herd so they can mate with his mares, but he's not going to give it to them."

She darted him a puzzled glance. "How do you know his name is Chief?"

"It came to me in a dream."

Sadie wasn't sure if Jarod was teasing her. "No it didn't." She started laughing.

The corner of his mouth twitched. It changed his whole countenance, captivating her. "He has a majestic bearing," he continued, "like Plenty Coups."

From her Montana history class she knew

Chief Plenty Coups was the last great chief of the Crow Nation. "Where do these horses come from?"

"They've lived here for centuries. One day Chief will be mine."

"Is that all right? I mean, isn't it against the law to catch one of them?"

A fierce expression crossed his face. "I don't take what doesn't belong to me. Because he's young, I'll give him another two years to get to know me. He saw me today, and he's seen me before. He'll see me again and again and start to trust me. One day he'll come to me of his own free will and eat oats out of my hand. When he has chosen me for himself, then it will be all right."

Sadie didn't doubt he could make it happen. Jarod had invisible power. A short time ago she'd thought she was going to die of sorrow, but that terrible pain had been lifted because of him.

That was the transcendent moment when Sadie's worship of Jarod Bannock began in earnest and she'd fallen deeply in love.

For the next three years Sadie had spent every moment she could steal out riding where she might run into him. Each meeting became more important to both of them. Once he'd started kissing her, they lived to be together and talked about marriage. Two days before her eighteenth birthday she rode to their favorite spot in a meadow filled with spring flowers—purple lupine and yellow bells. Her heart exploded with excitement the second she galloped over the rise near Crooked Canyon and saw him.

His black hair gleamed in the last rays of the sun. Astride his wild stallion Chief, he was more magnificent than nature itself. The stamp of his Caucasian father and Apsáalooke mother had created a face and body as unique as the two mountain blocks that formed the Pryor Mountains on both sides of the Montana-Wyoming border. Through erosion those mountains had risen from the prairie floor to eight thousand feet, creating a sanctuary for rare flora and fauna; a private refuge for her and Jarod.

She'd become aware of him as a child. As she'd grown older, she'd see him riding in the mountains. He'd always taken the time to talk to her, often going out of his way to answer her questions about his heritage.

His mother's family, the Big Lodge clan, had been part of the Mountain Crow division and raised horses. They were known as *Children of the Large-Beaked Bird.* Sadie never tired of his stories.

He told her about archaeological evidence of his ancestors in the area that dated back more than 10,000 years. The Crow Nation considered the "Arrow Shot Into Rock" Pryor Mountain to be sacred. Jarod had explained that all the mountain ranges in the territory of the Crow were sacred. He'd taught her so many things....

She looked around the meadow now. Two days before her birthday their talk had turned into a physical expression of mutual love. They'd become lovers for the first time under the dark canopy of the sky.

To be that close to another human, the person she adored more than life, filled her with an indescribable joy that was painful in its intensity. They'd become a part of each other, mind, heart and body.

She never wanted to leave him, but he'd forced her to go home, promising to meet again the next night so they could slip away to get married. He intended to be with her forever.

He pulled her against his hard body one more time, covering her face and hair in frenzied kisses. She was so hungry for him she caught his face in her hands and found his mouth.

After a few minutes he grasped her arms and held her from him. "You have to go home now."

"Not yet—" She fought to move closer to him, but he was too powerful for her. "My father will think I'm still at Liz's house studying for finals."

He shook his head. "We can't take any more chances, Sadie. You know as well as I do that with his violent temper your father will shoot me on sight if he finds out where you've been tonight. You need to go home now. Tomorrow night we'll leave for the reservation and be married. From then on you'll be known as Mrs. Jarod Bannock."

"Don't send me away," she begged. "I can't stand to be apart from you."

"Only one more night separates us, Sadie. Meet me here tomorrow at the same time. Bring your driver's license and your birth certificate. We'll ride over to the firebreak road where I'll have the truck and trailer parked. Then we'll leave for White Lodge.

"The next morning you'll be eighteen. We'll stop to get our marriage license. There'll be no waiting period. All you have to do is sign a waiver that you accept full responsibility for any consequences that might arise from failure to obtain a blood test for rubella immunity before marriage. That's it. After that we'll drive to the reservation."

She'd gone to the reservation with him several times over the years and once with his sister, Avery. Everyone in his Crow family had made her feel welcome.

"Remember—you'll be eighteen. I've made all the preparations for our wedding with my uncle Charlo. As one of the tribal elders, he'll marry us. There'll be at least a hundred of the tribe gathered."

"So many!"

"Yes. Our marriage is a celebration of life. You'll be eighteen and your father will have no rights over you by then."

She stared into his piercing black eyes. "What about your grandparents?" Sadie had loved Ralph and Addie Bannock the moment she'd met them. "How do you think they really feel about us getting married?"

"You have to ask? They're crazy about you. I've already told them our wedding plans. They're helping me any way they can. Earlier today my grandmother told me she can't wait for us to be living under the same roof with them until we can build our own place. Don't forget they loved your mother and like to think of you as the daughter they were never able to have. Surely you know that."

The words warmed her heart. "I love them, too." Sadie shivered with nervous excitement. "You really haven't changed your mind? You want to marry me? The daughter of the man who has hated your family forever?"

"Your father has something wrong in his head, but it has nothing to do with you." His dark brows furrowed, giving him a fierce look. "I made you an oath." He kissed her throat. "I've chosen you for my wife. How could you possibly doubt I want to marry you after what we've shared?"

"I don't doubt it," she said, her voice trembling. "You know I've loved you forever. Having you as my husband is all I've ever dreamed about. Oh, Jarod, I love you so much. I can't wait—"

He caressed her hair, which cascaded to her waist, and then his hands fell away. "Tomorrow night we'll be together forever. But you've got to go while I still have the strength to let you go."

"Why don't we just leave for the reservation now?"

"You know why. You're still seventeen and the risk of getting caught is too great." Jarod reached into his pocket and pulled out a beaded bracelet, which he fastened around her wrist. "This was made by my mother's family. After the ceremony you'll be given the earrings and belt that go with it."

"It's so beautiful!" The intricate geometric designs stood out in blues and pinks.

"Not as beautiful as you are," he said, his voice deep and velvety soft. "Now you have to go." He walked her to her horse. Once she'd mounted, he climbed on his stallion and rode with her to the top of the hill. They leaned toward each other for one last hungry kiss. "Tomorrow night, Sadie."

"Tomorrow night," she whispered against his lips.

Tomorrow night. Tomorrow night. Tomorrow night. Her heart pounded the message all the way home.

Remembering that night now, Sadie felt the tears roll down her face. Their love affair had turned into a disaster, permanently setting daughter and father against each other. She was forced to leave for California and never saw Jarod again. And the Hensons had been left to deal with their drunken boss until the bitter end. Guilt had swamped Sadie, but she'd had no choice except to leave the ranch to prevent her father from carrying out his threat to kill Jarod.

While her mind made a mental list of what to do first before she and Zane left for Montana, she hung up the phone and took a clean cloth to wash Ryan's face and hands. "Come on, sweetheart." She kissed his light brown hair. "Lunch is over. Time for a nap."

While she changed his diaper, she looked out the upstairs window of the house she'd lived in with her mother and Tim on Potrero Hill. The view of San Francisco Bay was spectacular from here.

But much as she loved this city where her

mother had been born and raised—where she'd met Daniel when he'd come here on business—Sadie was a Montana girl through and through. With her father's death, her exile was over. *She could go home.*

She longed to be back riding a horse through the pockets of white sweet clover that perfumed the land in the spring. Though she'd made friends in San Francisco and had dated quite a bit, she yearned for her beloved ranch and her oldest friends.

As for Jarod Bannock, eight years of living away from him had given her perspective.

He was a man now, destined to be the head of the Bannock empire one day. According to Liz he had a new love interest. Obviously he hadn't pined for Sadie all these years. And she wasn't a lovesick teenager who'd thought her broken heart would never heal after her father's treachery against Jarod. He'd been the one behind the truck accident that had put Jarod in the hospital. But that was ancient history now. She was a twenty-six-year-old woman who couldn't wait to take her half brother back to Farfields Ranch where they belonged.

Ryan might end up being her only child,

which made him doubly precious to her. One day Ryan Corkin Lawson would grow up and become head of the ranch and make it a success. In time he'd learn how to do every chore and manage the accounts. She'd teach him how to tend the calves that needed to be culled from the herd.

That had been Sadie's favorite job as a young girl. The sickly ones were brought to the corral at the side of the ranch house. Sadie had named them after the native flora: yellow bell, pussytoes, snowberry, pearly. Ryan would love it!

Before she left his room, she hugged and kissed the precious little boy. While she waited for Zane, she went into the den and phoned the Methodist Church in White Lodge, where she and her mother had once attended services.

In a few minutes she got hold of Minister Lyman, a man she didn't know. Together they worked out the particulars about the service and burial. The minister would coordinate with the Bitterroot Mortuary, where the hospital would transport her father's body.

To the minister's credit he said nothing negative about her father. He only expressed his condolences and agreed to take care of the service. After thanking him, she rang off and sat at the computer to start writing the obituary. She could do everything online. Within a couple of hours the announcement would come out in the *Billings Gazette* and *Carbon County News*. How should she word it?

On May 6, Daniel Burns Corkin of Farfields Ranch, Montana, passed away from natural causes at the age of fifty-three after being the cruelest man alive.

Too many words? On second thought why not make it simpler and put what the munchkins sang when Dorothy arrived in Oz.

"Ding Dong! The Wicked Witch is dead!"

"Hey, boss."

"Glad you came in the truck, Ben. I need you to get this new calf to one of the hutches before a predator comes after it. She has a broken foot from being stepped on." There was no need to phone Liz Henson, White Lodge's new vet. Jarod's sister, Avery, could splint it. "Would you help me put her in the back?"

"Sure." Together they lifted the calf, careful

not to do any more damage, but the mother bellowed in protest.

"I know how you feel," Jarod said over his shoulder. "Your baby will be back soon."

Ben chuckled. "You think she understands you?"

"I guess we'll find out the answer to that imponderable in the great hereafter." Jarod closed the tailgate and then shoved his cowboy hat to the back of his head, shifting his gaze to the new foreman of the Hitting Rocks Ranch. The affable manager showed a real liking for his sister, but so far that interest hadn't been reciprocated. Ben needed to meet someone else. "You were going to tell me something?"

"Avery sent me to find you. I guess your phone's turned off."

"The battery needs recharging. What's up?"

"She wanted you to know Daniel Corkin died at White Lodge Hospital early this morning of acute liver failure."

What?

Jarod staggered in place.

Sadie's monster father had really given up the ghost?

"The Hensons were with him. They got word to Liz and she phoned Avery."

The news he hadn't expected to come for another decade or more sent a great rushing wind through his ears, carrying painful whispers from the past that he'd tried to block out all these years. They came at him from every direction, dredging up bittersweet memories so clear they could have happened yesterday.

But Jarod managed to control his emotions in front of Ben. "Appreciate you telling me." After a pause he said, "If Avery can't tend to the calf, I'll call Liz. You go on. I'll follow on my horse Blackberry."

Ben nodded and took off.

Long after the truck disappeared, Jarod stood in the pasture to gentle the calf's mother, adrenaline gushing through his veins. Sadie would show up long enough to bury her father. Then what?

He threw his head back, taking in the cotton-ball clouds drifting across an early May sky. With Sadie's mother buried in California, it no doubt meant the end of Farfields. Sadie hadn't stepped on Montana soil in eight years. The note he'd received in the hospital after his

truck accident when she'd left the ranch had
been simple enough.

> *Jarod,*
> *You begged me to consider carefully the*
> *decision to marry you. I have thought*
> *about it and realize it just won't work.*
> *I'm going to live with my mother in Cali-*
> *fornia, but I want you to know I'll always*
> *treasure our time together.*
> *Sadie.*

For eight years Jarod had done his damned-
est to avoid any news of her and for the most
part had succeeded. *Until now...*

By the time he rode into the barn, twilight
was turning into night. He levered himself off
Blackberry and led him into the stall.

"You're kind of late, aren't you?"

Jarod couldn't remember when there wasn't
a baiting tone in Ned's voice. Out of the corner of his eye he saw the youngest of his four
cousins walking toward him. Ned's three siblings were good friends with Jarod.

He scrutinized Ned, who was a year
younger than him. Even that slight age differ-
ence upset Ned, but the rancor he felt for Jarod
ran much deeper for other reasons. They were

both Bannocks and lived in separate houses on the Hitting Rocks Ranch, but the fact that Jarod's mother had been a full Crow Indian was an embarrassment to the bigoted Ned. He liked to pretend Jarod wasn't part of the Bannock family and took great pleasure in treating him like a second-class citizen.

Ned was also still single and had always had a thing for Sadie Corkin, feelings that were never reciprocated. "It took me longer than usual to check out the new calves. How about you? Were you able to get the old bale truck fixed today or do we need to buy a new one?"

"If it comes to that, I'll talk it over with my dad."

Grant Bannock, Jarod's uncle, was a good man. But he had his hands full with Ned, who'd been spoiled most of his life and did his share of drinking. Jarod often had to keep a close eye on him to make certain he got his chores done. Not even Tyson Bannock, Ned's grandfather and Ralph's brother, could control him at times.

Ned had always dreamed of marrying Sadie Corkin and one day being in charge of both ranches. But that dream was in no one's interest but his own. Ralph Bannock, Jarod's grandfather, was the head of the ranch and his closeness to Jarod was like pouring salt on Ned's open wound.

Jarod patted the horse's rump before turning to his cousin. "Was there something else you wanted?"

Ned had looped his thumbs in the pockets of his jeans and stared at Jarod, who at six foot three topped him by two inches. Jarod saw a wild glitter in those hazel eyes that felt like hatred, confirming his suspicions that this encounter had to do with the news Ben had brought him earlier. Now that Sadie would be coming back for the burial, Ned wanted Jarod out of the picture.

"I thought you should know old man Corkin kicked the bucket early this morning."

Jarod didn't bother telling his cousin he was way ahead of him.

"If I were you," Ned warned, "I wouldn't get any ideas about showing my face at the funeral since he hated your guts." Jarod noted the heightened venom in his voice.

There'd been a lot of hate inside Daniel that had nothing to do with Jarod. In that regard Sadie's father and Ned had a lot in common, but no good would come of pointing that out to his cousin.

Jarod's uncle Charlo would describe Ned as an "empty war bonnet." The thought brought a faint smile to his lips. "Thanks for the advice."

Ned smirked. "No problem. Because of you there's been enough tension between the Corkins and the Bannocks. Or maybe you're itching to start another War of the Roses and manipulate your grandfather into buying Farfields for you. To my recollection that battle lasted a hundred years."

"I believe that was the Hundred Years War." Ned's ridiculous plan to acquire Sadie and the Corkin ranch in the hope oil could be found there was pitiable. "The War of the Roses lasted thirty years and the Scots only triumphed for ten of them. If my grandmother were still alive, we could check the facts with her."

Addie Bannock loved her history, and Jarod loved hearing what she could tell him about that part of his ancestry.

Even in the semidarkness of the barn, he detected a ruddy color creeping into Ned's cheeks. For once his cousin didn't seem to have a rebuttal.

"Do you know what's important, Ned? Daniel's death puts an end to any talk of war between the two families, for which we can all be grateful. I have a feeling this news will bring new life to both our grandfathers. Those two brothers are sick to death of it. Frankly, so am I. Good night."

As he walked out of the barn, Ned's last salvo caught up to him.

"If you think this is over, then you're as *loco* as Charlo." It sounded like a threat.

Jarod kept walking. Daniel Corkin's death had shaken everyone, including his troubled cousin Ned.

Chapter 2

"... And so into Your hands, O merciful God, we commend Your servant Daniel Burns Corkin. Acknowledge, we humbly beseech You, a sheep of Your own fold, a lamb of Your own flock, a sinner of Your own redeeming. Receive Daniel into the arms of Your mercy, into the blessed rest of everlasting peace, and into the glorious company of those who have gone before. Amen."

After the collective "amens," Minister Lyman looked at Sadie before eying the assembled crowd. She hadn't noticed the people who'd attended. In fact, she hadn't talked to anyone yet.

"While they finish the work here, Daniel's daughter, Sadie Corkin, and the Hensons, who've worked for Daniel all these years and are like a second family to Sadie, invite all of you back to the ranch house for refreshments."

The house, with the extraordinary backdrop of the Pryor Mountains, was only a two-minute walk from the family plot with its smattering of pine trees. Sadie had already ordered a headstone, but it wouldn't be ready for a few weeks.

She felt an arm slip around her shoulders. "Let me take Ryan for you so you can have some time alone."

When she looked up she saw Liz Henson, her dearest, oldest friend. They'd been like sisters growing up. Even while Liz attended vet school at Colorado State, they'd stayed in close touch. "Are you sure?"

"Of course I am." Liz kissed Ryan's cheek. "Since you flew in yesterday, we've been getting to know each other, haven't we?" She plucked him out of Sadie's arms. "Come with me, little baby brother, and I'll get you something to eat."

At first he protested, but eventually his voice grew faint. Liz had a loving way about her. Sadie knew he was in the best of hands.

Zane walked up to her. She saw the compassion in his blue eyes. "It was a lovely service. Your father is being laid to rest with all the dignity he would have wanted."

"He wanted Mother with him, but I'm glad she's buried with Tim. He brought her the joy she deserved in this life."

"You brought her joy the day you were born, and she'd be so proud you're raising Ryan. I plan to help you any way I can. I hope you know that."

"You're a wonderful man, Zane. Ryan is so lucky to have you in his life."

"He's a little Tim."

"I know. Those dimples get to me every time," she told him, smiling.

"Yup. Don't forget he's my life now, too!"

"As if I could forget."

Zane, she knew, had reached an emotional crossroads in his life and was still struggling to find himself. There'd been so many losses in his life, her heart went out to him. Thank heaven they had Ryan to cling to.

The afternoon sun caused Zane to squint.

"Everyone's gone inside the house. I'm going to help Liz. If you need us, you know where to find us."

She nodded. The mortuary staff was waiting for her to leave so they could lower the casket and finish their part of the work, but she couldn't seem to get up from the chair they'd brought for her. Since the phone call from Millie five days ago, her life had been a blur. She barely remembered the flight from San Francisco to Billings, let alone the drive in the rental car with Zane and Ryan to the ranch. Someone could use her for a pin cushion and she wouldn't feel a thing.

Sadie counted a dozen large sprays of flowers around the grave site. Such kindness for a man who'd made few friends humbled her. The huge arrangement with the gorgeous purple-and-white flowers kept attracting her attention. For as long as she could remember that color combination had been her favorite.

Needing to know who'd sent the floral offering, she stood and walked around to gather the cards. She recognized every name. So many people who'd touched their lives and had loved her mother were still here offering to help in any way they could. When she pulled out the insert from the purple-and-white flowers, her breath caught.

> *Sadie,*
> *Your mother and father's greatest blessing. Let this be a time for all hearts to heal.*
> *Love, Ralph Bannock and all the Bannocks—including the good, the bad and the ugly. Hope you haven't forgotten I'm the ugly one.*

She could hear Ralph saying it. He could be a great tease and she'd forgotten nothing.

A laugh escaped her lips as she put the cards in the pocket of her suit jacket. How she'd loved and missed him and Addie! Sadie had sent purple-and-white flowers when Addie had passed away, and today he'd reciprocated. She would have come for his wife's funeral if there'd been any way possible, but fear of what her father would do to Jarod if she came back had prevented her from showing up.

There could have been so much loving and happiness in her family, but her father's demons had put them through years of grief that affected the whole community. Suddenly she was sobbing through the laughter.

Needing to hide, Sadie hurried over to the granddaddy pine where she used to build nests of pine needles beneath its branches for the birds. She leaned against the base of the trunk while she wept buckets. How was she going to get through today, let alone tomorrow?

Her father's flawed view of life, his cruelty, had occupied so much of her thinking, she didn't know how to fill that negative space now that he was gone. She felt flung into a void, unable to get her bearings. And then she heard a male voice behind her. A voice like dark velvet. Only one man in this world sounded like that.

"Long ago my uncle Charlo gave me good advice. Walk forward, and when the mountain appears as the obstacle, turn each stone one by one. Don't try to move the mountain. Instead, turn each stone that makes up the mountain."

Jarod...

She hadn't heard that voice since her teens, but she'd recognize it if it had been a hundred years ago. His sister, Avery, had once told Sadie he was known in the tribe as "Sits in the Center" because he was part white and straddled two worlds of knowledge.

Since he'd just picked up on Sadie's tortured

thoughts, she couldn't deny he had uncanny abilities. But too many years had passed and they were no longer the same people. The agony of loss she'd once felt had been replaced by a dull pain that had never quite gone away. Wiping the moisture off her cheeks with the backs of her hands, she turned to face him.

He was a twenty-nine-year-old man now, tall and muscled, physical traits he'd inherited from his handsome father, Colin Bannock. But the short hair she remembered was now a shiny mane of midnight-black, caught at the nape with a thong. His complexion was bronzed by the sun and she picked out a scar near the edge of his right eyebrow she hadn't seen before. No doubt he'd received that in the truck accident that left him unconscious.

He wore a dark dress suit with a white shirt, like the other men, but there was something magnificent about his bearing. The powerful combination of his Crow and Bannock heritage meant no man was Jarod's equal in looks or stature.

She sensed a new confidence in him that had come with maturity. The coal-black of his piercing eyes beneath arched brows the same color sent unexpected chills down Sadie's spine.

The whole beautiful look of him caused her to quiver. Once she'd lain in his arms and they'd made glorious love. Did he ever think about that night and their plans to marry the day she turned eighteen?

After she'd fled to California, she'd prayed he would ignore the words in her note and call Millie. Once he'd left the hospital and got her number in California from the housekeeper, she'd expected his call so she could explain about the traumatic episode at the ranch with her father.

But Jarod hadn't called Millie, and there had been no word from him at all. Learning that he was out of the hospital and on his feet again, she'd prayed she would hear from him. But after a month of waiting, she'd decided he really was relieved they hadn't gotten married, so she hadn't tried to reach him.

That's when she'd given him another name: *Born of Flint.* The Crow nation referred to the Pryor Mountains as the Hitting Rock Mountains because of the abundance of flint found there, which they chipped into sharp, blade-like arrowheads. Jarod's silence had been like one of those blades, piercing her heart with deadly accuracy.

"It's good to see you again, Sadie, even if it's under such painful circumstances," he said. "Ned warned me not to show up, but my grandfather's been ill and asked me to represent him."

And if he hadn't asked you, Jarod, would you still have come?

"He's too tired to go out. Do you mind?"

Did she mind that Jarod's unexpected appearance had just turned her life upside down for the second time?

"Of course not. Liz told me Ralph has suffered recurring bouts of pneumonia. I love him. Always have. Please tell him the flowers he sent are breathtaking." She plucked a white-and-purple flower from the arrangement and handed them to him. "These are from me. Tell him I'll come to see him Tuesday evening. By then I'll be more settled."

He grasped the stems. "If I tell him that, then you have to promise you won't disappoint him. He couldn't take it."

She sucked in her breath. *You mean the way you disappointed me after you said you would always love me? Not one word or phone call from you in eight years about my note? Surely you knew there had to be a life and death reason behind it.*

"Sadie?"

Another voice and just in time.

She tore her gaze away from Jarod. Zane was walking toward her, holding a fussy Ryan. "Here she is, sport." The moment he put the little boy in her arms, Ryan calmed down. This child was the sunshine in her life.

Zane smiled at them. "He was good for a while, but with all those unfamiliar faces, he missed you."

Sadie clung to her baby brother, needing a buffer against Jarod, who stood there looking too splendid for words. She finally averted her eyes and kissed Ryan. "I missed you, too." She cleared her throat, realizing she'd forgotten her manners. "Zane Lawson, have you met Jarod Bannock, our neighbor to the east?"

He nodded. "Liz introduced us."

At a loss for words in the brief silence that followed, Sadie shifted Ryan to her other arm. "I'm sorry I left you so long, sweetheart. Come on. There are a lot of people I need to thank for coming."

She glanced one last time at Jarod over Ryan's head. "It's been good to see you, too, Jarod," she lied. Her pain was too great to be near him any longer. "Thanks for the wise counsel from your uncle Charlo. In truth I *have* come back to a mountain. Getting through the rest of this day will be like turning over that first stone."

As Jarod grimaced, Sadie hugged her brother harder. "Please give Uncle Charlo my regards the next time you see him. I always was a little in awe of him."

After eight years Jarod finally had his answer. She'd meant every word in the note she'd sent him. *Not one phone call or letter from her in all that time.* It appeared the sacred vow he'd made to her hadn't touched her soul.

Gutted by feelings he'd never experienced before, he watched the three of them walk back to the house. They looked good together, at ease with each other. Comfortable. Just how comfortable he couldn't tell yet. Was there something in the genes that attracted the Corkin women to the Lawson brothers?

But the girl he remembered with the long silky blond hair hanging almost to her waist was gone. Except for her eyes—Montana blue like the sky—everything else had changed. Her mouth looked fuller. She'd grown another inch.

Blue jeans and a Western shirt on a coltish figure had been replaced with a sophisticated black suit that outlined the voluptuous curves of her body. The gold tips of her hair, styled into a windblown look, brushed the collar of a lavender blouse. And high heels, not cowboy boots, called his attention to her long, beautiful legs.

There was an earthy element about her not apparent eight years ago. He hadn't been able to identify it until she'd caught the towheaded boy in her arms. Then everything clicked into place. She'd become a mother as surely as if she'd given birth. He'd seen the same thing happen in the Crow clan—they watched out for the adopted ones. The experience defined Sadie in a new way. It explained the hungry look in the uncle's eyes.

Jarod was flooded by jealousy, an emotion so foreign he could scarcely comprehend it, and the flowers meant for his grandfather dropped to the ground. Not wanting to be seen, he stole around the side of the ranch house and had almost reached his truck when Connor caught up to him.

"Jarod? Wait a minute! Where's the fire?"

His head whipped around and he met his younger brother's brown eyes. Connor had been through a painful divorce several years ago, but his many steer wrestling competitions when he wasn't working on the ranch with Jarod had kept him from sinking into a permanent depression. This past week he'd been away at a rodeo in Texas, but after learning about Daniel, he'd come home for the funeral.

"Avery and I looked for you before the service."

"My flight from Dallas was late. I just got here. Come inside with me."

That would be impossible. "I can't, but Avery will be glad to see you got here."

Connor cocked his dark blond head in concern. "Are you all right?"

Jarod's lungs constricted. "Why wouldn't I be?"

"I don't know. You seem…different."

Yes, he was different. The passionate, stars-in-her-eyes woman who'd made him feel immortal had disappeared forever.

"I promised grandfather I wouldn't be

long. He wants to hear about the funeral and know who attended. He has great affection for Sadie."

His brother nodded in understanding. "Don't we all."

"How's the best bulldogger in the state after your last event?" The question was automatic, though Jarod's mind was somewhere else, lost in those pain-filled blue eyes that had looked right through him.

"I'm not complaining, but I'll tell you about it later. Listen—as long as you're going back to the house, tell grandfather I'll be home as soon as I've talked to Sadie. How is she? It's been years since I last saw her."

A lifetime, you mean.

"She's busy taking care of her brother, Ryan." That shouldn't have made Jarod feel as if he'd been spirited to a different universe.

Connor shook his head. "It's incredible what happened to that family. Maybe now that Daniel's gone she'll have some peace. Avery told me on the phone she doesn't have a clue what Sadie's going to do now."

"I would imagine she'll go back to San Francisco with Ryan and his uncle."

Connor looked stunned. "Do you think the

two of them are…?" He didn't finish what he was going to say.

"I don't know."

"He's old enough to be her father!"

"He certainly doesn't look it, but age doesn't always matter." The way her eyes had softened when she'd looked at Zane Lawson had sent a thunderbolt through Jarod. "Why don't you go inside and make your own judgment. I've got to leave. Grandfather's waiting."

"Okay. See you back at the house."

But once Jarod had driven home, he went straight to his room and changed into jeans and a shirt. Before he talked to his grandfather, who was still asleep according to his caregiver, Martha, Jarod needed to expend a lot of energy.

He'd made tentative plans to have dinner in town with Leslie Weston after the funeral. She was the woman he'd been dating lately, but he couldn't be with her right now, not after seeing Sadie again. He would have to reschedule with her. For the moment the only way to deal with his turmoil was to ride into the mountains. He'd take his new stallion up Lost Canyon. Volan needed the exercise.

Though he started out in that direction,

midway there he found himself changing course. After eight years of avoiding the meadow, he galloped toward it as if he were on automatic pilot. When he reached their favorite spot, he dismounted and slumped into the bed of wildflowers. Their intoxicating scent was full of her.

Jarod remembered that last night with her as if it was yesterday. After their time together, he'd followed her to make sure she reached the Corkin ranch safely. He'd felt great pride that she rode like the wind. She and Liz Henson had provided stiff competition for the other barrel racers around the county, until Sadie suddenly quit. When Jarod had asked her about it, she'd said it had taken too much time away from being with him.

When he could no longer see her blond hair whipping around her, he'd set off the long way home, circling her property to avoid being seen. But before he'd reached the barn he'd had the impression he was being followed.

In a lightning move he turned Chief around and bolted toward the clump of pines where he'd detected human motion. As he moved closer he heard a curse before his stalker rode away, but Jarod had the momentum. He knew in his gut it was Ned. In half a minute he'd cut him off, forcing him to stop.

He looked at his cousin. "Where are you going in such an all-fired hurry this time of night?"

"None of your damn business."

"It's a good thing I knew it was you or I might have pulled you off Jasper to find out who's been keeping tabs on me. I would think you'd have better things to do with your time."

"You've been with Sadie." Ned's accusation was riddled with fury.

It was possible Ned had seen him and Sadie together tonight, but he decided to call his bluff, anyway. "If you know that for a fact, then why isn't my grandfather out here look-ing for me right now, waiting to read me the riot act? Wait, I've got an idea. Why don't you ride over to the Corkin ranch and ask Sadie to go for a midnight ride with you?"

When Ned said nothing, Jarod continued his taunting.

"Oh, I forgot. Her father forbid any Ban-nock to come near her years ago. Have you forgotten he vowed to fill us full of buckshot if he ever caught one of us on his property?

Of course, if you can figure out a way to get past Daniel, you can see what kind of reception you'll receive from her."

"Damn you to hell," Ned snarled as Jarod headed for the barn in the distance.

Grandfather would be furious with him for baiting Ned. It was a mistake he shouldn't have made this close to leaving with Sadie, but his cousin had chosen the wrong moment to confront Jarod, who was too full of adrenaline not to react.

For two cents he'd felt like knocking him cold. Ned had been asking for it for years, always sneaking around to catch him with Sadie. No doubt he planned to tell Daniel in the hope Sadie's father would finish Jarod off. For his grandparents' sake, Jarod had never stepped on Corkin property and he'd held back his anger at Ned. But Ned's obsession with Sadie seemed to be getting out of control.

Worse, Jarod couldn't get that night years ago out of his mind.

Once he'd removed Chief's saddle and had brushed him down, he entered the ranch house and found his grandparents in the den. That was the place where they always talked business at the end of the day. It was time to put his plans into action.

Addie hugged him. "I'm glad you're home. You missed dinner. Are you all right?"

"Yes. Everything is set for our marriage. Thank you for standing behind me in this."

"If your father were still alive, he'd understand and approve. We know it's the Crow way to marry young. You're a lot like your dad and have always known what you wanted."

"I'm thankful for your understanding and help, but right now my biggest concern is Ned. He must have been following me tonight. In order for him not to find out what's going on, I'm setting up a smoke screen. I'll pretend Chief is favoring his hind leg.

"After chores tomorrow I'll put Chief in the trailer and drive him to the clinic in White Lodge. If Ned finds out I paid a visit to Sam Rafferty for an X-ray, it should throw him off the scent long enough for us to be married."

"That's as good an idea as any," his grandfather said. "We decided not to tell Connor and Avery your plans. It's crucial they know nothing so that Ned doesn't pick up on any change in their behavior. He's a talker when he drinks and it could get back to Daniel."

Jarod nodded. "Where are they?"

Addie smiled. "Connor's in town with friends and Avery is spending the night with Cassie while they study for their finals. They'll be graduating from high school in two weeks."

"Sadie will be getting her diploma right along with them, but by then she'll be my wife. Here's what I'm going to do. After I leave the vet clinic, I'll drive up to the mountains where Sadie and I will meet. From there we'll go to the reservation to be married and spend a couple of days with Uncle Charlo and his family. We'll be home Sunday night in time for her to be back in school."

His grandfather got up from the chair and hugged him. "When you two arrive, we'll all celebrate."

Jarod's heart was full of love for his grandparents, who'd always supported him.

"Tell me what you need me to do before I leave tomorrow afternoon and I'll get it done."

"Why don't we go over the quarterly accounts after breakfast?" Ralph suggested.

"Sounds good."

He hugged his grandmother hard, then left the den and headed down the hall to the kitchen. After filling up on a couple of ham sandwiches and a quart of milk, he took the stairs two at a time to his bedroom at the top.

His watch said twenty after ten. At this time tomorrow night he'd be with Sadie on reservation property. He knew a private spot where they wouldn't be disturbed. They'd stay there until it was time to drive to White Lodge for their marriage license.

You're going to be a married man, Bannock.

If he had one regret it was that his siblings wouldn't be there. But when he brought Sadie home as his wife, they'd understand the measures he'd had to take to protect Sadie from her out-of-control father.

"So, Dr. Rafferty, you don't think there's a need to take an X-ray?" Jarod asked, walking Chief out of the trailer to the paddock behind the clinic with the vet.

"Not that I can see," Sam Rafferty told him.

"His limp does seem to be a lot better. Last night I was really worried about him."

"Horses aren't that different from people. Sometimes we wake up in the morning and everything hurts like hell. But the next day, we feel better."

"Well, I'll take your word for it nothing serious is wrong."

Sam nodded. "Give him a day of rest and see how he does."

"Will do. How much do I owe you?"

"Forget it. I didn't do anything."

"You can't make a living that way." Jarod put a hundred dollar bill in the vet's lab coat pocket. "Thanks, Doc."

"My pleasure." They shook hands before he led Chief back into the trailer and shut the door.

Jarod started the truck and drove his rig away from the clinic. Out of the corner of his eye he saw Ned's Jeep down the street across from the supermarket. That was no coincidence—Ned must still be tailing him.

Twenty after five. The sun would set at nine. Jarod would have driven to the mountains immediately, but he couldn't do that with Ned watching him. It would only take a half hour to reach Sadie. He had three hours to kill. Might as well drive Ned crazy.

After making a U turn, he parked near the supermarket and went in to buy a meal at the deli. Then he took it out to the truck and sat there to eat while he listened to music. Ned had finally disappeared, but Jarod knew he was somewhere nearby watching, hoping to see Sadie show up and join Jarod. The fool could wait till doomsday but he'd never find her here.

The sun sank lower until it dropped below the horizon. It was time to make his move. His heart thudding in anticipation of making love to Sadie for the rest of their lives, Jarod started the truck and turned onto a road that would eventually lead to the fire road. From that crossroads you could either go to the mountains the back way or head the other way for the reservation.

But as he reached the crossroads, from out of nowhere, something rammed him broadside. The last thing he heard was the din of twisting metal before he passed out.

The next day he woke up in the hospital with a serious brain concussion, bruises and a nasty gash near his eye. Frantic, he tried to reach Sadie, but the report from the Hensons came back that she wasn't at home.

When he awoke a second time, the nurse

brought him Sadie's note and read it to him.
The words ripped him to pieces.

Jarod lay in the clover remembering the
pain until Volan nudged him. Feeling as if his
heart weighed more than his body, he climbed
on the stallion and rode home.

Avery confronted him in the tack room
after he returned. Her brunette hair and bright
smile reminded him of their father Colin's
second wife, Hannah. She'd been a wonderful mother to Jarod, never pushing him. Avery
was a little more aggressive in that department.

"When you didn't come in the ranch house
with Connor, I knew you'd gone riding. Did it
help?" Her hazel eyes studied him anxiously.

She could read most of his moods, but he
didn't answer her this time. There was no help
for the disease he'd contracted eight years ago.

"Grandfather was hoping to talk to you."

"I know. I'll go see him now."

"He's gone to bed, but don't worry, Connor and I told him all we could. Great Uncle
Tyson came to the funeral with his family. It
was so strange, all of us together on Corkin
land after so many years of being warned off

the property. I think it overwhelmed Sadie. She thanked us for coming, but clung to her little brother the whole time."

Jarod's thoughts were black. "Did Ned behave?"

Her mouth tightened. "Does he ever?"

"Tell me what he did."

"He asked a lot of questions in such bad taste it raised the hairs on the back of my neck."

"Like what?"

At his rapid-fire question, his sister looked startled. "I was standing by them when he asked if she and Zane had an interest in each other besides Ryan. He said he hoped not because he was planning to spend a lot of time with her now that she was back."

Jarod bit down so hard he almost broke a tooth.

"It was appalling, but no one else heard him. Sadie didn't answer him, but I was so angry I broke in on their conversation. That angered Ned and caught Uncle Grant's attention. He wasn't thrilled with his son's behavior, either, and got him out of there as fast as he could."

"Ned gave me an ultimatum the other night."

"What kind?"

"Not to show up at the funeral."

"That's no surprise. He was jealous of you from birth. It only grew worse when grandfather gave you more responsibilities for running the ranch. Ned couldn't handle it. But when you and Sadie became friends, that killed him."

"There's a sickness in him."

"I know. Sadie was never interested in any of the guys chasing after her, least of all Ned. He used to wait for her after school and follow her as far as Corkin property. Sadie never paid him one whit of attention because the only guy she could ever see was *you*."

Until Jarod had planned to make her his wife. Then she'd run like the prong-horned antelope, putting fifteen hundred miles between them. Had his accident been the excuse she'd been looking for not to marry him?

"After today she'll like him even less, but I guess it doesn't matter," Avery added.

He closed his eyes tightly. "Why do you say that?"

"The chances of her having to deal with

him are pretty remote. She's got a home in California and a little brother to raise."

"With Zane's help?" Jarod didn't want to listen to another word.

"Forget what you're thinking. I asked her outright if she was involved with Zane. She said no and was shocked at the question. I think it actually hurt her."

Jarod's relief had him reeling.

"I have to tell you I'm envious of her. Ryan's such an adorable boy, I wish he were mine."

Those were strong words. Jarod heard wistfulness in her voice and eyed her with affection. "Your time will come, Avery."

Her eyes darted him a mischievous glance. "Are you trying to make me feel better, or did you have a vision about your only female sibling who's getting older?"

Her teasing never bothered him. He rubbed his lower lip absently. "I don't need a vision to know you're not destined to be alone. Ben's been crazy about you ever since he was hired."

Avery rolled her eyes. "That has to work both ways, big brother. If anyone ought to know about that, it's you. You're pushing thirty and until two months ago you had no prospects despite the fan club you ignore. Am I wrong or at long last has a woman finally gotten under your skin? Leslie's an extraordinary person, the kind I've been hoping you would meet."

"You and grandfather." But Jarod was too conflicted over Sadie to get into a discussion about anything. She'd just inherited Farfields, a place she'd loved heart and soul. Jarod couldn't imagine her leaving the land where she'd been born. But he'd been wrong about her before. Maybe she was involved with another man in California.

When are you going to learn, Bannock?

Chapter 3

It was Tuesday morning. Sadie had slept poorly and got up before Ryan, who was sleeping in the crib Millie had used for Liz. Zane had been installed in the guest bedroom and was still asleep. Though she'd come to the ranch to bury her father and take stock of her new situation, seeing Jarod after all these years had shaken her so badly, she was unnerved and restless. Through her friendship with Liz, she knew he hadn't married yet, though that made no sense when he could have any woman he wanted.

But recently Liz had dropped a little bomb

that over the past few months he'd been seeing an archaeologist working in the area named Leslie Weston. Liz seemed to think it was more serious than his other relationships had been.

Her breath caught. *Had they made love? Were they planning to marry?* Sadie couldn't bear thinking about it.

From her bedroom window she watched Liz leave the Hensons' small house adjacent to the ranch house and head for her truck. No doubt she was on her way to work at the Rafferty vet clinic in White Lodge. Pretty soon quiet-spoken Mac followed and started out for the barn to get going on his chores.

With a deep sigh, Sadie turned away and headed for the bathroom. Once she'd showered and washed her hair, she pulled on jeans and a cotton sweater. After blow-drying her hair and applying lipstick, she felt more prepared to face this first day of an altered life and turn the second stone.

To stay busy she fixed breakfast, woke and dressed Ryan for the day and then returned to the kitchen. She piled some cushions on one of the kitchen chairs for Ryan as Zane joined them to eat. Before the day was out, she'd take her dad's pickup and run into White Lodge for a high chair and a new crib.

Though she had everything she needed back in California, it would take time to ship her things here. While she was at it, she'd also buy some cowboy boots and start breaking them in.

Millie appeared at the back door. The housekeeper still had a trim figure and worked as hard as ever to keep the ranch house running smoothly. Her brown eyes widened in surprise when she walked into the kitchen and found the three of them assembled there. "Good morning, Millie. Come on in and eat breakfast with us." It was long past time someone waited on her for a change.

The older woman kissed Ryan's head before sitting next to him. "I think I'm in heaven."

"Good. You deserve to be waited on." Sadie brought a plate of bacon, eggs and hash browns to the table for her.

No sooner had Sadie started to drink her coffee than they heard a knock on the front door. She jumped up from the table. "That'll be Mr. Varney. I'll show him into the living room. He's here to talk about the will."

The attorney from Billings had come to the

graveside service and told her he'd be by on Tuesday morning.

"I'll take care of Ryan," Zane offered.

"Thank you." She got up and kissed her little brother's cheek. "I'll be back soon."

She hurried down the hall to the front room of the three-bedroom L-shaped ranch house. The place needed refurbishing. According to Mac, in the last few years her father had been operating Farfields in the red. He'd ended up selling most of the cattle. Toward the end he'd been too ill to take care of things and there'd been little money to pay Millie and Mac. The value of the ranch lay in the land itself.

Reed Varney had put on weight and his hair had thinned since the last time she'd seen him. He must be sixty by now and had handled her father's affairs for years. The man knew all the ugly Corkin secrets, including the particulars of the divorce, which was okay with Sadie since it was past history.

"Come in, Mr. Varney." She showed him into the living room. A couple of the funeral sprays filled the air with a fragrance that was almost cloying. Mac had taken some of the other arrangements to their cabin. "Would you care for some coffee?"

"No thanks." For some odd reason he wouldn't look her in the eye. She had the impression he was nervous.

"Then let's sit to talk." She chose one of the leather chairs opposite the couch where he'd taken a seat. As he opened his briefcase to pull out a thin file she asked, "How soon do you want to schedule the reading of the will?" For all their kindness, Mac and Millie should head the top of the list to receive the house they'd been living in all these years. She couldn't wait to tell them.

He rubbed his hands on top of his thighs, another gesture that indicated he felt uncomfortable. Sadie started to feel uneasy herself.

"Something's wrong. What is it?"

After clearing his throat he finally glanced at her. "The will is short and to the point. You can read it now. The particulars are all there." He handed her the file.

She blinked. Maybe her father had been in more financial trouble than she'd been led to believe. Taking a deep breath, she started to read. After getting past the legal jargon she came to her father's wishes.

*Mac and Millie Henson betrayed my
trust on my daughter's eighteenth birthday. Therefore they'll receive no inheritance, nor will my daughter, whom I've
disowned.*

*Over the years several people have
wanted to buy the ranch, but so far they
haven't met the asking price. I have their
offers on record. If no one else makes
an offer within a month of my death,
then the ranch and all its assets including my gun collection will be sold to the
highest bidder through Parker Realty in
Billings, Montana. My horse, Spook, has
been sold.*

*No furnishings are to be touched. The
new buyer will either use or dispose of
them. Under no circumstances can the
ranch be sold to a Bannock.*

Sadie gasped and jumped up from the chair.
Her father had lived to drink, hunt and hate
the Bannocks with a passion. The meanest
man alive didn't begin to describe him. Forget
the fact that he'd disowned her. When she'd
left for San Francisco, she never dreamed he'd
take out his fury on the Hensons like *this.*

"Does this mean he's thrown Mac and Millie out with nothing?" Her eyes filled with tears. "After all they've done for him over the years? The care they gave him toward the last?"

Varney eyed her with grave concern before nodding. "However, Mr. Bree at the realty firm has asked that the Hensons stay on to manage things until the new buyer takes ownership. It's entirely possible Mac Henson will be asked to continue on as foreman for the new owner."

Daniel had died nine days ago. In less than a month from now the eighty-five-acre ranch would be sold? She couldn't take it in. Her father wanted her and the Hensons off his land as fast as humanly possible. When he'd told her to get out eight years ago, he'd meant for it to be permanent. "What is the sale price?"

"Seven hundred thousand. He was in a lot of debt."

Her mind was madly trying to take everything in.

"What about me, Mr. Varney? Am I supposed to clear out today?"

With a troubled sigh, the older man got to his feet. "Legally you have no right to be here, but morally this is your home and you can stay until the new owner takes up residence. As for your own personal possessions, you're free to take them with you. I'm sorry, Sadie. I wish it could be otherwise. To be honest, I dreaded coming here today. You don't deserve this."

Reeling with pain, she walked him to the door. "It's Mac and Millie I worry about. The ranch is their home, too. I can hardly bear it."

When Jarod hadn't showed up that night eight years ago, the Hensons were the ones who had tried to comfort her. She'd believed he had decided at the last minute that he couldn't go through with their marriage, and she would never have survived if they hadn't been there to help her get through that ghastly night.

Reed Varney shook his head. "When Daniel summoned me to the ranch, I begged him not to do this, but he was beyond reason."

She stared into space. "He's always been beyond reason." This proved more than ever why her mother had been forced to abandon Sadie.

If Eileen had stayed in the marriage, who knew what would have happened during one of his drunken rages when he'd threatened to kill his wife. Eileen's decision to let him keep Sadie had probably saved both their lives.

When Sadie had found out about Jarod's accident, her father had threatened to kill Jarod if she went to the hospital to be with him. He'd made her write a letter telling Jarod she never wanted to see him again and then he'd told her to get out of his house. Millie and Mac were afraid for her life and urged her to leave Montana and go to her mother in California, saving her once more.

"Thank you for coming," she said quietly to the lawyer.

"Of course. The number for Parker Realty is listed on the paper. They've already put an ad in the multiple listings section. Things should be moving quickly. I'll be in touch with you again soon."

The second he left, she grabbed the file and hurried to her bedroom to hide it in the dresser drawer. She never wanted the Hensons to know what he'd put in the will about them. They'd been wonderful surrogate parents to her. Somehow she had to protect them.

With that decision made, she grabbed her purse and left for the kitchen, determined to lie through her teeth if she had to. She found

Millie at the sink and gave her a hug. "Hey! I made the mess and planned to clean it up."

"Nonsense. How did everything go?"

"Fine. Tomorrow I'll drive to Billings and meet with him in his office," she lied. "Where's Zane?"

"Outside with Ryan. If Tim Lawson was as terrific as Zane, then your mother was a very lucky woman."

"She was. So was I, to be raised by you and Mac. I love you and Liz dearly. You know that, don't you?"

"The feeling's mutual."

"You're my family now and that's the way it's going to stay." *No matter what she had to do.*

"Nothing would make us happier." They hugged again.

"I'm going to drive into White Lodge. Do you want me to do any shopping for you while I'm there?"

"We stocked up for the funeral so I think we're fine right now."

"Okay. See you later. Just so you know, tonight I'm going to visit Ralph Bannock. Zane will babysit Ryan." She hadn't asked him yet, but knew he'd do it.

Zane's wife had betrayed him with another man while he'd been in the navy. After he'd left the military, they'd divorced and, not long after, Zane had lost his elder brother, Tim. "Honey, I can do that."

"I know you can, Millie, but you spent enough time raising me. The last thing I want to do is take advantage of you. We'll be back shortly."

Sadie reached for the truck keys on the peg at the back door and hurried outside. She found Zane walking around with Ryan. He made the perfect father. His ex-wife had been the loser in that relationship. Sadie knew how much he'd wanted a family. It broke her heart.

She scooped her little brother from the ground before darting Zane a glance. "Will you drive me to town? We need to talk."

"Sure."

She handed him the keys to her father's Silverado and walked over to get in. They'd brought a car seat from California for Ryan and had already installed it in the backseat. Once he was strapped in securely, she climbed into the front with Zane and they took off.

Zane gave her a sideways glance. "I know that look on your face. You've had bad news."

"Much worse than anything I had imagined, but Mac and Millie don't know a thing yet. The fact is my father disowned me." She ended up telling him everything written in the will. "I've got three weeks from today to come up with a plan. I don't want the Hensons to find out about this."

"Of course not. That monster!" he muttered under his breath, but she heard him. "I'm sorry, Sadie." They followed the dirt road out to the highway.

"Don't be. With him, the shoe fits. The bottom line is, if I want to make my home on this ranch, I'll have to buy it from the Realtor in Billings. There was no mention in the will that I couldn't. I have some savings after working for your brother, but not nearly enough to make a dent. In the meantime I need to find a job in town and put Ryan in day care."

Zane grimaced. "I could give you some money."

"You're an angel, Zane, but you gave your ex-wife the house you both lived in, so you need to hold on to any money you've saved. I'll have to find another avenue to pay off the debt owing the bank so I can hold on to the ranch, but I've got to hurry."

"I've got an idea how you can do it." She jerked her head toward him, waiting for the miracle answer. "I could sell Tim's house in San Francisco."

Sadie made several sounds of protest. "After your divorce, mother willed it to you before she died because she assumed I'd inherit the ranch one day. She knew Tim would have wanted you to have it."

"You're forgetting she expected you to go on living there with Ryan."

"But it's not mine, and I don't want to live in San Francisco."

"Neither do I. I have no desire to be anywhere near my ex, so I've got another idea."

"What?"

"The house isn't completely paid off, but I could still get a substantial amount if I sell it. With that money, plus any you have, we could move here and become joint owners of the ranch."

Her heart gave a great clap. "You're not serious!"

"Yeah. Actually, I am. I spent a lot of years in the military and know I won't be happy unless I'm working outdoors in some capacity. So far I haven't found a job that appeals to me. I can help with the ranching for a while until I know what it is I want to do with the rest of my life."

"Zane, you're just saying that because you're at loose ends and are one of the great guys of this world."

"I'm saying it because I have no parents, no brother and I don't want to lose Ryan. I know you have nothing holding you in California. To be honest, I like the idea of being part owner with you. It'll be our investment for Ryan's future."

Her eyes smarted with unshed tears. "If you're really serious…"

"I'm dead serious. Take a look around. With these mountains, this is God's country all right. It's growing on me like crazy. I already like Mac and Millie. And the little guy in back seems perfectly content. Why don't you think about it?"

"I *am* thinking. So hard I'm ready to have a heart attack."

"Don't do that! If you wake up tomorrow and say it's a go, I'll fly back to San Francisco and get the house on the market. While I'm there, I'll put everything from the house and my apartment in storage for us. What do you say?"

She was so full of gratitude, she could hardly talk. "I say I don't need to wait until tomorrow to tell you yes, but I don't want ownership. The ranch should be put in your name for you and Ryan. I'll get a job and do housekeeping to earn my keep. In time we'll build up a new herd of cattle. Anything less and I won't agree."

He flashed her the kind of smile she hadn't seen since before Tim's death. Zane had dimples, too, an irresistible Lawson trait. "You sound just like your mother when she's made up her mind, but you need to think about this. There's a whole life you've left behind in San Francisco. Men you've dated. Friends."

"I know, and I've enjoyed all of it including my job at your brother's store. But with Mother gone, it hasn't been the same. Now that my father has died, I feel the only place I really belong is here."

After a period of quiet he said, "I can tell you this much. I feel this ranch growing on me."

Like Sadie, Zane needed to put the painful past behind him and get on with life.

"Tell you what, Zane. When I drive you to the airport tomorrow, I'll stop by Mr. Varney's office and let him know we have a plan for you to buy the ranch. He can inform the Realtor and we'll go from there."

"Sadie—" There was a solemn tone in his voice. "If things don't work out, we'll find another small ranch for sale around here. Montana is in your blood. We won't let your father win."

She had no words to express the depth of her love for him. Instead, she leaned across the seat and kissed his cheek.

On Tuesday night Jarod had just returned from the upper pasture when he caught sight of Daniel Corkin's Silverado parked in front of the Bannock ranch house. *Sadie was still here.* The blood pounded in his ears as he let himself in the side door of the den on the main floor. His grandfather's room was farther down the hallway of the two-story house.

With Connor headed for another rodeo event in Oklahoma, either Avery or their housekeeper, Jenny, would have let her in. He planted himself in the doorway of the den. When Sadie left, she would have to walk past him to reach the foyer. Since it had grown dark, he didn't imagine he'd have to wait much longer. His grandfather tired easily these days.

As if he'd willed her to appear, he saw light and movement at the end of the hall. She moved quietly in his direction. When she was within a few feet he said hello to her.

"Oh—"

"Forgive me if I startled you, Sadie. How's my grandfather?"

She stepped back, hugging her arms to her waist. He saw no sign of the vivacious Sadie Corkin of eight years ago who'd caused every male heart in Carbon County to race at the sight of her.

When he'd watched her galloping through the meadow, blond hair flying behind her like a pennant in the sunshine, he'd hardly been able to breathe. The moment she'd seen him, she'd dismount and run into his arms, her hair smelling sweet from her peach-scented shampoo.

Without losing a heartbeat, he'd lay her down in the sweet white clover and they would kiss, clinging in a frenzy of need while they'd tried to become one. Just remembering those secret times made his limbs grow heavy with desire.

"He fell asleep while we were talking," she answered without looking at him directly. "I'm afraid I wore him out."

"That means you made him happy and left him in a peaceful state. When I had breakfast with him this morning, he was excited to think you'd be coming by. He was always partial to you and Liz." He almost said his grandfather had been waiting to welcome her into the Bannock family, but that would be dredging up the past.

"I care for him a lot." She shifted nervously. "I'm afraid I have to get back to Ryan now, so don't let me keep you. Good night." She darted away like a frightened doe spooked by a noise in the underbrush.

He'd promised himself to stay away from her, but the trail of her haunting fragrance drove him to follow her out the front door to the truck. By the time she'd climbed behind the wheel, he'd reached the passenger side. Not considering the wisdom of it, he got in and shut the door.

"What are you doing?" She sounded panicked.

Jarod forced his voice to remain calm. "Isn't it obvious? We have unfinished business, Sadie. While we're alone, now is as good a time as any to talk." He stretched his arm along the back of the seat, fighting the urge to plunge his hand into her silky hair the way he'd done so many times in the past. "To pretend we don't have a history serves no purpose. What I'm interested to know is how you can dismiss it so easily."

"I've dismissed nothing," she said, her voice shaking, "but sometimes it's better to leave certain things alone. In our case it's one stone that shouldn't be turned."

"I disagree. Let's start with that note you had delivered to me at the hospital. That was quite a turnaround from the night before when you'd promised to marry me. Or have you forgotten?"

"Of course not." She stirred restlessly. "I waited for you until dark, but you never came."

"Ned had been stalking me in town."

"Ned?"

He nodded. "I had to wait until I saw his Jeep disappear before I headed out to get you."

She struggled for breath. "I didn't know

that. I was afraid to be out any longer in case my father realized I wasn't home or at Liz's, so I headed back. I thought you'd decided not to come, after all," she said in a barely audible voice.

"*Not come?* I was on my way to you when a truck blindsided me. Everything went black. A hiker found me and I didn't wake up until I was taken to the hospital in an ambulance. By then it was afternoon the next day. I couldn't reach you on the phone. Late that night one of the nurses brought me your note."

He felt her shudder.

"What happened, Sadie? For weeks I'd been asking you if you were sure about marrying me. You had every opportunity to turn me down before I went to the trouble of preparing for our wedding. Surely I deserve a better explanation for you not showing up than the pathetic one you sent me."

Her head was still lowered. "I—I'm afraid to tell you for fear you won't believe me," she stammered. "I've kept this a secret for so long, but now that my father is dead, you need to hear the truth."

He gritted his teeth. "Why didn't you tell

me before?" he rasped. "It's been eight hell-ish years, Sadie."

"You think I don't know that?" She whipped her head around to face him. "I didn't hear about the accident until late the next day when Mac told me. The second I found out, I started out the door to go straight to the hospital. But that's when my father stopped me. He said if I went near you, he would kill you."

Jarod frowned. "Kill me? He'd been threatening to kill any Bannock that came near you on his property for years, always when he'd had too much to drink. Why did you suddenly believe him?"

"This time was different!"

He blinked. "Start at the beginning and don't leave anything out."

"After Mac told me about your accident, he gave me the keys to his truck so I could drive to the hospital. I left the house, but my father followed me out and forbade me to leave. I told him I was going to see you and he couldn't stop me. I was eighteen and he had no more right to tell me what to do. But before I could climb into the cab, he said something that made my blood run cold."

Jarod waited.

She stared at him in the semidarkness. "He warned me that if I ever went near you again, another accident would happen to you and you wouldn't survive it."

"What?"

Jarod's thoughts reeled.

"I was afraid you wouldn't believe me." She started to open the door to get out, but Jarod was faster and reached across to stop her.

He knew Daniel Corkin was demented when he got too drunk, but— "Are you saying he drove the truck that ran me down the night before?" Jarod caught her shoulder in his grasp, bringing their mouths within inches of each other.

"No." Sadie shook her head, unable to hold back the tears. "But my father had to be behind the accident. Otherwise why would he have said that? He probably paid someone to drive into you, and after all these years, that person is still out there."

Was it true?

He gripped her shoulder tighter. "I *knew* it wasn't a simple accident. When I felt that kind of force on a dirt road with no one else around, I thought it had to be a small plane making a forced landing that ran into me.

"It all happened too fast for me to see anything. The impact caused the truck to roll into the culvert and twisted the horse trailer onto its side. The police said it had to have been a truck, but after an exhaustive investigation, they couldn't find the person responsible."

Sadie moaned. "It was so horrific. I heard that Chief was injured, too."

"Yes, but he survived."

"Thank heaven. I don't know how, but someone knew we were planning to get married and word got back to my father. Maybe someone from the reservation did some talking in town. Oh, Jarod." She broke down, burying her face in her hands. "You could have been killed."

She was right about that.

"I can't bear to think about that night. There was evil in my father. I realized he *would* kill you another time given more provocation. At that point I did the only thing I could do and promised not to see you again. He made me write that note and then he told me to get out of the house and stay out. He obviously assumed I'd run to the Hensons."

Jarod heard her words, but it took time for him to absorb them.

"I was so terrified to learn you were in the hospital, and so terrified of him, I knew I had to get away and stay away. All these years I've wondered who could have done something so sinister to you. My father must have paid that man a lot of money he didn't have."

He sucked in a breath. "Whether your father was bluffing about the accident or not, his objective of separating us was accomplished. You were gone out of my life as if you'd never been there."

"Please listen to me, Jarod. In the note I wrote, those words were only meant to convince my father. How could you have believed them? I was going to be your wife!"

He stared her down, unable to fathom what had happened. Something didn't ring true, but he'd have to think long and hard about it first. He slowly released her arm.

"Just tell me one thing. Why did you go to your mother after she'd abandoned you for all those years? It made no sense. I couldn't come up with any conceivable explanation, so I finally had to conclude you couldn't bring yourself to marry me."

"Jarod," she pleaded, "I don't know how you could think that! When you didn't come and I still knew nothing about your accident, I thought you'd changed your mind about getting married, or maybe your uncle had urged you to put off the marriage for a while longer. I wanted to die when you didn't show up. Mac and Millie came in my room to try to calm me down. You have no idea what was going on inside me that night."

"That made two of us. I lay on that hospital bed incapacitated with no way to talk to you. My grandparents thought we were on the reservation enjoying our honeymoon."

"I didn't know that!" she half cried. "I was so upset Mac and Millie told me a secret they'd been keeping from me because my father had sworn them to secrecy. If they broke that oath, he would have thrown them off the property. Millie said the only reason they hadn't left him was because of me."

He shook his head in disbelief. "What secret?"

"They told me he'd threatened to kill my mother if she tried to take me away from him. Jarod, all those years I thought she didn't love me, but it was just the opposite. She always wanted me, grieved for me. She kept in touch with the Hensons every day to find out how

I was. But they had to keep quiet because of my father."

"Is that the truth?"

"Yes, but I didn't know it until that moment."

Jarod rubbed the side of his jaw. "A mother's love," he murmured. "You wanted it more than you wanted me."

"No, Jarod. You have everything wrong."

"I don't think so," he argued. "When you heard about my accident, it was obvious you didn't want to be my wife or you would have found a way to get in touch with me at the hospital. You knew that when I got out, I'd come for you and we would have gotten away from your father. I wasn't afraid of him."

"But I *was!* He'd just admitted he would make sure you were dead if I so much as looked at you. I couldn't bear that, so I went to my mother. Don't forget he'd threatened her years earlier. My father was capable of anything! With a gun or a rifle in his hand, he was lethal. Since I'd turned eighteen, Mac and Millie urged me to get away from my father and go to her because he was out of control. Mac drove me to Billings."

Jarod felt as though a giant hand had just

cut off his breath. "So you let Mac do that instead of driving you to the reservation where my uncle would have taken care of you until I got out of the hospital. You promised to love me forever."

He could barely make out her words she was sobbing so much. "You were my life, Jarod, but when I never heard from you after you recovered, I thought you didn't want me. I thought my life was over. Don't you understand? I was devastated to think you'd decided it wouldn't be wise to marry me because of my father. He hated you—hated all the Bannocks. You have to believe that the only reason I left was so my father wouldn't hurt you again."

A boulder had lodged in his throat. "How could you think that when I was prepared to be your husband and take care of you? I swore I would protect you. Do you honestly think I would have let him or anyone else hurt either one of us?"

"He managed it the first time."

Jarod's features hardened. "Why don't you tell me the real reason why you ran away from me? I'm warning you. I won't let you go until I get the truth out of you."

Tears rolled down her cheeks. "I *have* told you, but you're so stubborn you refuse to listen."

"You think I haven't listened? Did Ned get to you, after all?"

"No!" She sounded wild with anger. "I couldn't stand Ned. He revolted me."

"But he told you about my father, didn't he?"

She stared at him through the tears. "What are you talking about?"

"After all this time and all we've been through, are you still going to pretend you don't know the truth?"

"What truth?" she cried.

"My mother and father were never married."

Stillness fell around them.

"They weren't? I swear I've never heard any of this. Ned used to call you a bastard and a half-breed under his breath, but I knew he was insanely jealous of you. He had such a foul mouth, my friends and I always ran from him when he followed us around."

Sadie's earnestness shook him.

"Jarod Bannock, are you trying to tell me

you think I heard about your parents and was ashamed to become your wife?"

Jarod struggled to hide the guilt rising up in him.

"You *do* think it! I can see it on your face. How dare you think that about me!"

"That's exactly how it was," he returned angrily. "You were playing a game with me— the half Indian. But you were a teenager then, living through a lot of pain and turned to me. I was three years older and should have known better than to believe you and I shared something rare."

"We did," she whispered, her voice throbbing. "Can't you understand that I was convinced my father would kill you?" Even in the semidarkness her face had lost color. "Listen to me, Jarod. I'm going to tell you something right now.

"Even if I knew about your parents, I was ready to live with you no matter what because I *loved* you. *I* was the one who begged you to take me away before I turned eighteen. Remember? I didn't care. I would have hidden out on the reservation with you. That's how deeply in love I was with you. So don't you dare credit feelings and motives to me that were never mine."

Gutted after what he'd heard, Jarod needed to get out of the truck. He started to open the door, but she grabbed his arm. "Oh, no, you don't! We're not through yet. I want to know why you never, ever told me the truth about your parents."

Jarod realized he couldn't avoid this conversation any longer. While he tried to find the words, she launched her own.

"It seems to me your cousin did a lot of damage I didn't know about, otherwise you wouldn't have held anything back from me. What did he tell you? That a white girl would never want you once she knew the truth? He got under your skin, didn't he? Well, we're alone now, so I want to hear the whole truth. You owe me that much before you walk away again."

He deserved that much and closed his eyes tightly before sitting back.

"Dad was twenty when he drove to the reservation to look at the horses. The Crow loved their animals and knew good horse flesh. My uncle Charlo showed him around. While they were talking, his younger sister Raven came riding up on a palomino. Dad told me she looked like a princess. He was so taken by her, he forgot about the horses. From then on he kept driving over there and finally told Charlo he wanted to marry her.

"My uncle told him she was destined to marry another man in the clan, but by that time Raven was in love with my father. At that point Charlo took him to meet their mother. Her word was law. She said her daughter was old enough to make up her own mind. They spent that night together on the reservation. It meant they were married. There was no ceremony. I was conceived that night."

"Oh, Jarod." She sniffled. "What a beautiful story. Did they live on the reservation?"

"On and off. Dad took her home to meet my grandparents. They loved my father and welcomed Raven. When she discovered she was pregnant, she spent more time with her family. I was born on the reservation. But Addie had prepared a nursery, so I lived in both places.

"That winter my mother caught pneumonia, and though my grandfather paid for the best health care, she died within six weeks of my birth and was buried on the reservation. My father was grief-stricken. It was hard to take me out to the reservation as often after that because of all the reminders.

"My Bannock grandparents helped raise me. Eventually Dad met Hannah at church and they married, then Connor and Avery were born. That's the whole story. Though secretly I knew Great Uncle Tyson's family didn't approve of what my father had done, they were never unkind to him or to me."

"Except for Ned," Sadie muttered. "He's as intolerant as my father. The fact that you're an exceptional man only makes your cousin angrier."

"There's more to it than that, Sadie. After my parents were killed in a freak lightning storm, Ned became more vocal about his hate for me and my background. He constantly tried to show me up. It grew uglier with time. But *you* were the crux of the problem. He wanted to go out with you himself, and I knew it.

"When I used to watch you compete at the rodeo, I knew Ned was in the crowd, wishing you'd go home with him after it was over. I loved knowing you and I had secret plans to meet later. I had too much pride knowing it was I you wanted."

She shifted in the seat. "I lived to be with you. That's why it kills me to think that Ned was able to undermine your faith in me once I left Montana. I had to write what I did in that note to sound believable to my father, but I can't believe you didn't read between the lines. I waited for weeks, months, years, hoping and praying I'd hear from you so I could tell you everything and we could make plans to meet."

"That works both ways, Sadie. I waited weeks for a phone call from you. Maybe now you can understand how devastated I was when you fled to your mother instead of marrying me.

"But after you'd gone to California and time passed, I realized you were right to escape me. Despite the Bannock name, I'll always be treated as a second-class citizen by certain people. If you had married me, you would have been forced to deal with the kind of prejudice Ned dishes out on a daily basis."

They'd reached an impasse. He opened the door. "Eight years have passed. You've suffered some great losses in your life and now have a child to raise. I only wish you the best, Sadie."

Her features hardened. She wiped the moisture off her face. "If you can accuse me of being afraid to be your wife after all we shared, then you never knew me. I gave you a lot more credit than that. Have you forgotten the evening we met in the canyon and I told you about a lesson we'd had on the Plains Indians and the great Sioux Chief Sitting Bull?"

"Vaguely." Jarod knew he'd always been so excited to be with her, he'd barely taken in everything she'd told him.

"That lesson changed my view of life, but it's obvious you need a reminder of how deeply it touched me. Did I tell you our teacher made us memorize part of Sitting Bull's speech before the Dawes Commission in 1877? I still know it by heart and got an A for it."

Jarod had had no idea, but he nodded.

"Sitting Bull said, and I quote, 'if the Great Spirit had desired me to be a white man, he would have made me so in the first place. He put in your heart certain wishes and plans, and in my heart he put other and different desires. It is not necessary for eagles to be crows.

"'I am here by the will of the Great Spirit, and by his will I am chief.

"'In my early days, I was eager to learn and to do things, and therefore I learned quickly.'

"'Each man is good in the sight of the Great Spirit. Now that we are poor, we are free. No white man controls our footsteps. If we must die, we die defending our rights.

"'What white man can say I ever stole his land or a penny of his money? Yet they say that I am a thief. What white woman, however lonely, was ever captive or insulted by me? Yet they say I am a bad Indian.

"'What white man has ever seen me drunk? Who has ever come to me hungry and left me unfed? Who has seen me beat my wives or abuse my children? What law have I broken?

"'Is it wrong for me to love my own? Is it wicked for me because my skin is red? Because I am Sioux? Because I was born where my father lived? Because I would die for my people and my country? God made me an Indian.'"

When she'd finished, Jarod sat there in absolute wonder, so humbled he couldn't speak.

"You don't know how many times I wanted to face my father and Ned and deliver that speech to them," Sadie told him. "I wanted to yell at them, 'God made you men white and

Jarod's mother an Indian. So be thankful you were made at all and learn to live together!

"That speech made me love you all the more, Jarod. I can't believe you didn't know that. But as you said, it's probably that pride of yours. It's turned your heart to flint and stands in the way of reason.

"Do you know I've given you a second Crow name now that you've grown up? It's Born of Flint."

Born of Flint? That's what she thought of him? Everything was over.

"I wish you a safe journey back to California, Sadie."

Chapter 4

When Sadie walked through the back door of the ranch house Tuesday night, Millie was in the kitchen making coffee. She glanced at Sadie and said, "You look as bad as you did that night eight years ago. It can only mean one thing. Sit down and talk to me before you fall down, honey. Ryan's asleep and Zane's in his bedroom doing work on his laptop."

"Oh, Millie..." She ran into those arms that had always been outstretched to her. They hugged for a long time.

"You saw Jarod."

Sadie nodded and eased away. "I don't think it was by accident."

"No. He knew you were going to visit Ralph."

"He followed me to the truck. We talked about that ghastly night eight years ago. He said he couldn't come to the meadow until after dark because Ned had been stalking him in White Lodge. That's why he was so late."

"That doesn't surprise me one bit. Ned was always up to no good."

"But it was a revelation to me! When he thought it was safe, he started for the mountains but got broadsided by a truck." She told Millie everything they'd talked about.

"Don't tell me you didn't believe him—" The tenderness in her brown eyes defeated Sadie.

"Of course I believed him," she half protested. "But back then I was dying inside. Now it is eight years too late. Millie—" She scrunched her fists in anger. "All these years I've wanted to hate him for not trying to get in touch with me."

Millie's voice was gentle. "You didn't reach out to him, either. It's a tragedy you both lost out on eight years of loving. Ah, honey...you were so young, struggling with too many abandonment issues. When he didn't come for you in California, the pain was too much for you."

"You should have heard him, Millie. He... he thought I left Montana because I didn't want to marry a part Indian. Did you know his parents got married on the reservation? But no one knew about it, certainly not Ned.

"I didn't realize Jarod suffered so much from Ned's taunting. He *had* to know none of that mattered to me. Can you imagine him believing I thought less of him because of his heritage?"

The housekeeper gave her a sad smile. "Yes. Jarod is a proud man like his uncle Charlo. But at twenty-one, everything was on the line for him. Don't forget your father's hatred of the Bannocks, let alone his hatred of anyone who wasn't of pure English stock.

"Wanting to marry you was a daring dream for any man, but as we both know, Jarod was always his own person. In his fearless way he loved you and reached out for you. But when you left Montana before he got out of the hospital, all those demons planted in his mind by your father and Ned caused his common sense to desert him for a while."

"I see that now," Sadie whispered, grief stricken. "But I was afraid my father would kill him."

"Don't you know about the great wounded warrior inside him? He needed you to believe in him, to believe he would protect you."

"You're right."

"Did you tell him tonight that you'd wanted to marry him more than anything in the world?"

Sadie wiped her eyes with the palms of her hands. "Yes, but he didn't listen. Do you know what he said? In that stoic way of his he wished me a safe journey back to California."

Millie studied her for a moment. "Perhaps he thinks you and Zane are romantically involved. Have you forgotten that fierce Apsáalooke pride so quickly? According to my daughter, Zane Lawson is the most attractive man she's seen around these parts in years."

"No, Millie. I cleared that up with Avery the other day when she asked about Zane. She's close to Jarod and would have told him." But Ned had been brazen enough to ask her about Zane.

Millie shrugged. "Maybe Jarod thinks you're involved with a man in San Francisco and are looking forward to getting back to him."

"It never happened."

"All I can say is, if you're going to be neighbors with the Bannocks again, it wouldn't hurt to mend a fence that doesn't need to stay broken. Don't you agree? After all, Jarod's involved with another woman right now."

Pain pierced her. "I know. Apparently it's more serious than his other relationships."

"That doesn't surprise me. He's not a monk and he *is* getting to the age where a man wants to put down roots with a wife and children. Honey? Since you're not going back to California, perhaps you could tell him there is no other man in your life the next time you see him. If either one of you had done that eight years ago with a phone call or a letter, you might be the mother of one or two little Bannocks by now."

Except at that point in time, Millie hadn't known that Daniel was the person behind Jarod's accident, and still didn't. Sadie's father had talked to her outside where no one else could hear them. The horror of knowing her father would kill Jarod with little provocation was another secret she'd wanted to keep from the Hensons.

But the mention of one or two little Bannocks had Sadie swallowing hard. She'd entertained that vision too many times and suffered the heartache over and over again.

Sadie thanked Millie and said good-night. She tiptoed into the bedroom. Ryan was sound asleep, snuggled beside his blanket.

Good old Millie. Her sage advice nagged at Sadie as she got ready for bed. To mend that fence by telling Jarod there was no man in her life meant turning over the next stone. If she did tell him, she didn't know if she had enough courage to deal with the rejection of the grown man he'd become.

"Honey?" Millie peeked in her room. "I need to give you something. Now that you know the truth about that night, you should have this back." She handed Sadie the beaded bracelet Jarod had given her the night they'd made love and planned their future.

Sadie stared at the bracelet in disbelief. "I thought I'd lost it. You kept it?"

"Of course. I knew there had to be an explanation why he didn't meet you, but you were too wild with pain to hear me. When you took that bracelet off your wrist and tossed it across the room, I picked it up and put it away for safekeeping.

"Don't you know he would never have given you a gift like that if he hadn't loved you with all his soul? Jarod's a great man, Sadie. After you left, I cried bitter tears for both of you for years."

Sadie stared at the woman who'd been her mother through those difficult years. "What did I ever do to deserve you? I'll love you and Mac forever."

"Ditto. We couldn't have more children. You were a blessing in our lives, a sister for our Liz. We all needed each other."

Yes. Sadie wouldn't have made it without the Hensons.

She pressed the bracelet against her heart and fell asleep reliving that night in the mountains. *Jarod...*

So she *was* leaving the ranch. The Sadie he'd once known had gone for good.

Jarod stood outside the ranch house for a long time. The sound of Sadie's truck engine echoed in the empty cavern of his heart, the one she'd likened to flint.

When he'd checked on his grandfather and found him asleep, he'd told Jenny he was going to drive out to the reservation to see Uncle Charlo and would be back by tomorrow afternoon. Again it meant putting Leslie off, but it couldn't be helped.

He'd met the good-looking, redheaded archaeologist from Colorado through Avery. The two women worked at the dig site near Absarokee, Montana, run through the University in Billings. They were unearthing evidence of Crow history. Leslie's looks and mind had attracted him enough to start dating her, but seeing Sadie again made it impossible for him to sort out his feelings.

The reservation crossed several county lines with ninety percent of the population being farthest away in Big Horn County at the Crow Agency. However his uncle resided in the small settlement on the Pryor area of the reservation in Carbon County, only an hour's drive from the ranch.

If Martha needed anything, she could call his uncle Grant. But if there was a real emergency, he could come right back.

* * *

After spending the night on the reservation, Jarod drove straight to the ranch on Wednesday to look in on his grandfather. Since his hospital stay the month before, Ralph's condition could change on a dime because of the pneumonia plaguing him. Martha had just served him his lunch. She smiled at Jarod as he walked into the bedroom.

"I'll stay with him while he eats," he told her.

"He's in better spirits than I've seen him in a long time."

Jarod figured that might have had something to do with the visit from the gorgeous blonde on the neighboring ranch. Being with her last night had shaken him, though he wasn't sure in such a positive way.

You were my life, Jarod, but I thought you didn't want me. I thought my life was over. I was devastated to think you'd decided it wouldn't be wise to marry the daughter of Daniel Corkin. He hated you.

Even though he'd talked to his uncle, it had taken until early morning before the cloud over Jarod's mind had dispersed and he'd allowed himself to dig deeper for answers. Daniel wasn't the only person who'd hated Jarod enough to cause him injury. He could think of another man who matched that description.

A member of his own family.

Since Sadie's return to Montana, Ned had shot him glances that said he'd like to wipe Jarod off the face of the earth. Ned had always been up to trouble and had taken it upon himself to be chief watch dog of Jarod's activities. Was it possible he'd heard about Jarod's plans to marry Sadie?

Jarod couldn't imagine it, but if that was the case, then he understood the hate that could have driven Ned to prevent the ceremony from taking place. Couple that with his drinking and a scenario began to take form in Jarod's mind.

"I'm glad you're here, son," Ralph Bannock said. "We need to talk."

His grandfather's raspy voice jerked him from his black thoughts to the present. Since Jarod's father's death, his grandfather, whose thinning dark hair was streaked with silver, had started calling Jarod "son." Though he and Jarod were the same height, his grandfather had shrunk some. He was more fragile these days, and there were hollows in his cheeks.

He was propped against a pillow, sipping soup through a straw. Martha kept him shaved and smelling good. Today he had on the new pair of pajamas Connor had brought him.

Jarod spied a newly framed five-by-seven photograph placed on the bedside table. His breath caught when he realized it was a picture of his grandfather and Sadie taken when she couldn't have been more than six or seven. She was a little blond angel back then, sitting on the back of a pony.

His grandfather's eyes misted over when he saw where Jarod was looking. "Sadie gave me that last evening. I remember the day her mother brought her over to see the new pony. Addie took a picture of us and gave it to her. Sadie said that was one of the happiest memories of her life and wanted me to have it…. With that father of hers, she didn't have many good ones. There was always sweetness in that girl."

No one knew that better than Jarod. He'd never forgotten the day they'd rode into the rugged interior of the Pryors to find one of the wild horse herds. They'd come across a mare attending her foal, their shiny black coats standing out against the meadow of purple lupine. He and Sadie had watched for several hours. "I wish that little foal was mine. I never saw anything so beautiful in my life, Jarod."

The scene was almost as beautiful as Sadie herself. That was the day their souls joined.

Jarod knew in his gut Leslie Weston was becoming more serious about him, yet he kept holding back. It wasn't fair to her. She'd invited him to Colorado to meet her family, but he wasn't there yet.

When Sadie left again for California, maybe that would be the spell-breaker for him. So far no other woman had ever gotten past the entrance to that part of him where Sadie lived. She was his dream catcher, trapping the memories that would always haunt his nights.

Last night his uncle had listened to him before giving him a warning. "Consider the wolf that decides it is better to risk death for some chance of finding a mate and a territory than to live safely, but have no chance of reproduction. You don't know how many winters the Great Spirit will grant you, but they will be cold if you continue to torture yourself with insubstantial dreams that give no warmth."

Jarod knew his uncle was right. He could see a marriage working with Leslie. While he ranched, she'd be able to continue with her career. Together they'd raise a family. For a variety of reasons he felt she'd make a good wife. But would he make a good husband? The answer to that question was no. Not if he couldn't tear Sadie out of his heart.

"Son? Did you hear me?"

His head reared. "What was that, grandfather?"

"I said I need you to do me a favor."

"Anything." He sat in the chair next to the bed, emotionally shredded.

"It turns out Daniel is worse in death than he was in life."

Jarod sat forward. After what Sadie had told him about her father, he wasn't surprised. "What do you mean?" Sadie's father had cast a pall over their lives for too many years.

"He cut Sadie and the Hensons out of his will."

The news shocked Jarod. She'd said nothing of this last night. He shot to his feet. "But there's no one else to inherit!"

"That's right. On June third, the ranch is to be sold to the highest bidder. Parker Realty in Billings is handling it."

So soon? That was only two weeks away. Jarod's hands formed fists.

The lunatic was selling the place rather than give it to his own flesh and blood?

"I would buy it," his grandfather continued, "but Daniel thought of that, too. No Bannock will be able to touch it."

"But Sadie loves that ranch. It's her home. If nothing else, she'd want to keep it in her family."

"She told me she plans to buy it so she and the Hensons can live on the property until they die. It would be just like that lowlife Corkin to force her to come up with her own money to buy it back. You and I know her heart has always been here."

Jarod felt his heart skip a beat. Despite what everyone had been thinking, Sadie wasn't going back to California. Even when the circumstances pointed otherwise, deep down *Jarod had known.*

"Does she have the kind of money it will take?"

"She has savings, but Zane is flying back

to California to sell the Lawson house. That money combined with hers ought to be enough to pay off the bank loan so they can hold on to it until they come up with more."

"'They'?" His nervous system received another shocking jolt. "What does Zane have to do with her ranch?"

"Everything! Being Ryan's uncle, he has decided to move here with her. Together they're going to do the ranching."

Jarod frowned. "Does he know anything about ranching?"

"She said he's a retired navy SEAL who just got divorced after finding out his wife was unfaithful. If he was courageous enough to defend our country and survive thirteen years in the military, it stands to reason he can learn. Mac will be there to help him."

His grandfather had an amazing way of humbling Jarod.

"One day she wants it to be Ryan's in honor of Eileen. Their mother put her heart and soul into that ranch before Daniel drove her away. What I want you to do is pay a visit to our attorney in Billings. Ned wants that ranch. He wants Sadie, too, but she was never his to have."

Their eyes locked. His grandfather's steel-gray ones stared at him. "If it wasn't for that accident, she would have been your wife!"

As if Jarod needed to be reminded.

"When Ned hears it's on the market, he'll try to fight the will on the grounds that a third-party designee won't stand up in court these days and anyone can buy it. I want you to get to Harlow before Ned does. Inform him of Sadie's desperate plight and make sure no one else gets their hands on her property. Block him with everything you've got." His gray eyebrows lifted. "I mean *everything*."

Jarod got the message. This was a mission he was going to relish. Ralph Bannock of the Hitting Rocks Ranch was a big name in the State of Montana and wielded a certain amount of power among the business community. For once Jarod planned to use that power for leverage.

"Don't worry about Tyson or your Uncle Grant," his grandfather continued, unaware of the tumult inside Jarod. "I'll take care of them. If they decide the blood between them and Ned is thicker than the blood between them and me, then there will be war. We'll have to get there before they do. Time is of the essence. I'll be damned if I'll let Daniel Corkin cheat Sadie out of her rightful inheritance. Addie wouldn't have stood for it."

Jarod remembered Ned's angry warning in the barn two nights ago about the war not being over. Little did his cousin know what he was in for. Though Ralph had always been Jarod's champion, until this moment he hadn't known how much he loved his grandfather. "I'll drive to Billings first thing in the morning."

"We'll keep this under wraps."

"I'm way ahead of you."

Since Thursday was Liz's day off from the clinic and she wanted to tend Ryan, Sadie had to wait till then to drive Zane to Billings to make his flight. Little Ryan cried when they walked out the back door. They both felt the wrench, but Sadie knew he'd be laughing in a few minutes.

After she dropped Zane off at the airport, Sadie met with Mr. Bree at Parker Realty and they talked business. He couldn't tell her about the other bids, but he did give her a price. If she could meet it, he'd be happy to sell the property to Zane.

She explained about the house in San Francisco, advising that Zane's agent would contact Mr. Bree with a notice of intent to use the money from the sale of the house to purchase the ranch. Everything depended on a quick sale. Sadie put down earnest money from her savings account. With that accomplished, she left his office and headed back to the ranch. She had a lot to discuss with Zane when he called her later.

Ryan was taking his afternoon nap when she returned. Now was a good time to get busy cleaning out her father's bedroom. So far she hadn't been able to bring herself to go in it. When she told Liz and Millie of her intentions, they wouldn't hear of it.

"Give it more time, honey," Millie urged her. "While Ryan's still asleep, why not put on those sassy new cowboy boots and take a ride on Sunflower?"

"She's a lot like Brandy once was," Liz commented. "Playful, with plenty of spirit. You'll love her. But Maisy's energetic, too. Go ahead and ride whichever one you want."

"Thank you." Sadie stared out the living room window facing the mountains. "I presume Dad sold my horse after I left."

"Along with half the cattle."

"Did he get rid of my saddle, too?"

"No. It's still waiting for you in the tack room." Millie got up from the couch and put an arm around her. "Don't dwell on the past. I happen to know a girl around here who never let a day go by without going for a ride."

Obviously, Millie knew she was on the verge of breaking down.

"Maybe for a half hour. If you're sure."

"What else have we got to do? Having a child in this house makes me feel useful again."

"It makes me want one of my own," Liz said on a mournful note.

So far every subject they'd touched on was painful one way or the other. "I'll get ready, but I won't take a long ride. If Ryan starts crying for me, call me on my cell."

Millie shook her head. "Whatever did we do before cell phones?"

If Sadie and Jarod could have called each other eight years ago...

But Sadie's father had forbidden her to have a phone. He didn't want guys calling her without him knowing about it. At Christmas, four months before she'd fled to California, Jarod had bought her one and paid for the service, but she'd been too afraid her father would find out. She'd made Jarod take it back.

If they'd been able to talk before his accident, she would have known he hadn't deserted her. They would have communicated while he was in the hospital and their marriage would have taken place the second he got out....

You're a fool to dredge up so much pain, Sadie.

She put the phone she'd bought ages ago in her blouse pocket, then went in the bedroom to change into her cowboy boots. Just a short ride to the bluff overlooking the ranch and back.

After thanking Millie and Liz, she left the house through the back door and walked to the barn, lifting her face to the sun.

The smell of the barn flooded her with bittersweet memories. Horses had been her soul mates, just as Jarod had said. When her mom had left, this was the place where she'd come to cry her heart out and find solace. They's always listened and nudged her as if to say they understood.

Though the fights between her parents had stopped, for a long time the emptiness of no loving parent in the house had swallowed her alive. From her earliest memories, her father had been a gun-toting alcoholic. He'd always been gruff, though her mother had done her best to shield Sadie from him.

But somewhere along the way he'd turned hard and cold. After the divorce he'd just have to look at Sadie and she'd known he was seeing her mother. Sadie had learned to stay out of his way.

A neigh from the horse in the barn startled her, breaking her free of those memories. She discovered her cheeks were damp. After wiping the tears away, she walked over to Maisy's stall. The sorrel stared at her as if surprised to see a stranger.

Sadie moved on to Sunflower's stall. With a yellowish gray coat set off by a black mane and tail, the dun-colored mare was well named. She nickered a greeting.

Sadie rubbed her nose. "Well, aren't you the friendliest horse around here. Want to go for a ride? I know you're one of Liz's horses, but you won't care if I take you out for some exercise, right?" She marveled that her friend, who'd become a vet, was still Montana's champion barrel racer. But as she'd informed Sadie, this would be her last year of competition and she hoped to go to the Pro Rodeo Finals in Las Vegas in December.

The horse nickered again, bringing a smile to Sadie. She could saddle and bridle a horse in her sleep, and before long she had left the barn and was galloping away from the ranch. As the horse responded to her body language, the exhilaration she hadn't felt in years came rushing back. She'd done this before. She'd felt this way before.

Her inner compass told her where to go. She was on one of those rare highs and discovered herself racing toward the rocky formations in the distance where Jarod had first taken her to see the wild horses. Sadie knew he wouldn't be there. She didn't even know if the horses still ran there, but she was back now and this was one pilgrimmage she had to make.

In a few minutes she'd reached the place where her bond with Jarod had been forged. The deserted gulch held no evidence that anything had ever happened here, but cut Sadie open and you'd see his imprint on the organ pumping her life's blood.

Jarod. It was always you. It will always be you.

when Jarod told Harlow's secretary he needed to see his grandfather's attorney ASAP, he figured he might have to wait hours or come back the next day. But the two men were old friends. As soon as she buzzed her boss and told him who was out in reception, she smiled at Jarod.

"He says you can go right in."

"Thanks, Nancy." He walked across the foyer to the double doors and opened them.

Harlow started toward him. Though the older man was in his seventies and had a shock of white hair, he was a wiry, energetic individual. His shrewd blue eyes played over Jarod with genuine pleasure. "Come on in! It's always good to see you."

They shook hands before the lawyer took a seat behind his desk, motioning for Jarod to sit in one of the leather wing-backed chairs in front of it. "Has Ralph taken another turn for the worse?"

"His last bout of pneumonia left him weak, but he's still fighting."

"That's good to hear. And Tyson?"

"His macular degeneration along with ulcers has taken a real toll." The brothers were only two years apart. "I've come on my grandfather's behalf about something vital."

"Ralph appears to be depending on you more and more to run the Hitting Rocks Ranch. He couldn't choose a better man to be following in his footsteps."

Jarod's uncle Grant probably wouldn't like hearing that, but Jarod had always liked Harlow and felt the man's sincerity. "They're big ones."

Harlow chuckled. "Indeed they are." He pushed a stack of legal briefs to the side of his desk and leaned forward. "Tell me what's going on."

It didn't take Jarod long to explain the problem.

The older man touched his fingertips together. "What a tragedy, but there is a very simple way around the problem. If Ralph wants to make certain Sadie Corkin doesn't lose her ranch without her knowing he's behind it, I'll act as a straw buyer and purchase the property."

"It's going for $700,000."

He nodded. "When all the papers are filed and transactions made, Ralph can pay me and the land will be deeded over to Zane Lawson. He can work out the details with Ralph to get him paid back. No laws have been broken, therefore no grounds for a court case. That part of Daniel Corkin's will doesn't hold water. Anyone has the right to buy that ranch including a Bannock."

With those words Jarod felt his chest expand. Only a friendship as strong as the one his grandfather and Harlow had built over the years could have achieved this miracle. "How soon could you act on it?"

"Today if you want." He quirked one white eyebrow. "You're anticipating a bidding war?"

"According to Sadie, who confided in my grandfather, two other people made offers on the property before Daniel died. The place will be sold to one of them if no other offers come in before the deadline. The ranch is already in the multiple listings online. I'm afraid once my cousin sees it, he'll outbid anyone else to make make sure he comes out on top."

"Which cousin is that?"

"Ned."

"Ah, yes. Grant's son, the one who's always been in trouble. Why would he want to buy that ranch?"

"Though close to a century has gone by without any evidence, Ned still believes there's oil on the land. He's determined to get his hands on it." *And on Sadie.*

"Do you know how many gamblers have squandered their lives going after that same pipe dream around these parts?"

"Ned has never been able to let it go," Jarod said.

"From what Ralph told me," Brigg mentioned, "that cousin of yours has some deep-seated problems. I recall hearing about the time when he and his friend were caught stealing some wild horses on federal land. It cost Grant plenty to keep that hushed up."

Jarod's brow furrowed in surprise. "I didn't know that. What happened?"

"Instead of ending up in jail, they were charged with drunk and disorderly conduct. It took influence with the judge and a lot of money to keep that under wraps. Ralph said

Ned's father was continually bailing him out of some pretty nasty scrapes."

This was all news to Jarod. For Ned to have that kind of serious brush with the law underlined his cousin's dark side. Jarod had no idea his grandfather had confided in Harlow to this extent.

He winked at Jarod. "We'll get there before Ned does. I'll phone Mr. Bree at Parker Realty after you leave and set things in motion."

"When my grandfather hears that news, it'll probably add several years to his life."

The lawyer smiled. "I owe him so many favors for sending business my way, I'm delighted to do this."

"We're indebted to you, Harlow. Sadie's been our neighbor since she was born. It's time she had some joy in her life." He stood to shake the lawyer's hand.

Harlow squinted at him. "I'll give you and Ralph a ring as soon as I've spoken with Mr. Bree."

"Good. I'll see myself out."

On the way to the underground car park, Jarod mulled over the new revelation about Ned. It triggered his memory to the time his cousin had accused him of stealing Chief.

Though Jarod had gotten legal permission to keep the wild horse once he'd tamed him, Ned had been furious. Having always been in competition with Jarod, Ned might have decided to steal a wild horse to prove he could have one of his own, too.

Since Sadie had come back, his toxic behavior around Jarod had an edge of desperation that bordered on instability.

Ever since his accident, Jarod had wanted to know the identity of the person who'd intentionally tried to take him out. Sadie believed her father had been behind it. So much so that she'd left the state to protect Jarod. But if it had been Daniel, he would have arranged a series of accidents long before that night. Over the years Jarod had occasionally seen Sadie's father out hunting in the mountains. He could have picked Jarod off at any time.

He suspected that Daniel had used the accident as an excuse to frighten his daughter further, knowing how vulnerable she was at that point. The man had been born with few scruples, but he'd stopped short of murder, only threatened it.

When Jarod really thought about it, there was only one person he was aware of who truly hated him for personal reasons. That was his cousin…

The revelation coming from Harlow had made him see things in a different light. More and more he was convinced that his cousin was the guilty party and had gotten away with his crime for years now.

On the night in question, Ned must have arranged for a truck ahead of time, probably from one of the friends he hung around with when they went off to keg parties. After driving his Jeep around town to throw Jarod off the scent, he'd gotten that friend to drive him to the crossroads where he'd ambushed Jarod. Or maybe Ned had borrowed it and was alone when he drove into Jarod.

Needing evidence, Jarod decided to visit some auto paint and body shops while he was still in Billings.

Before Ned had returned the borrowed truck to the owner, he would have gone to a shop for repairs, but not in White Lodge, where the police had already done a search.

When he reached his truck, Jarod bought a hamburger at a drive-through before starting his investigation of the dozens of body and paint shops in Billings. The police had checked a few places here, but they could have missed some. Most places kept invoices, accounts payable/receivable ledgers and expense reports for a minimum of seven years, but generally longer. Sadie's birthday had been May tenth, a Thursday. That narrowed the field as to time.

It was a long shot, but he might come across a business that had done some work for Ned. He would have used an assumed name and paid cash.

One by one he interviewed the service managers, hoping to come up with a lead. No one could give him information on the spot. He left his cell phone number for them to call him and also used his phone to retrieve a photo of Ned from the ranching office information for the managers to download.

Tomorrow morning he'd leave early for Bozeman and go through the same process. It wouldn't take as long to cover since it was a third the size of Billings, a city with a population over 100,000.

On his way home, his cell phone rang. Hoping it was one of the body shops, he clicked on without looking at the Caller ID and said hello.

"Hi!"

His hand tightened on the wheel. It was Leslie. For the life of him he couldn't muster any enthusiasm at hearing her voice. The only emotion at the moment was guilt that he couldn't give her what she wanted. "Hi, yourself."

"Is this a bad time to call?"

"No. I've been going nonstop and am just leaving Billings to drive back to the ranch. How was your day? Any new finds?"

"A hide scraper made out of bottle glass."

Jarod nodded. "Sounds like traditional technology meshed with a modern material."

"Exactly. I'd love you to work with me one of these days. Am I going to see you tonight?"

He'd already put her off once. "Let's do it. I'll meet you at the Moose Creek Barbecue in White Lodge at seven for dinner. You can tell me what else you've found."

"I can't wait to see you."

Jarod didn't feel the same way. "It'll be good to see you, too. I've had a ton of business to do for my grandfather and will enjoy the break."

"Jarod?" she asked tentatively. "Are you all right?"

He took a labored breath. "Why do you ask?"

"I don't know. You sound...detached."

"It's not intentional. I'm afraid it has been a long day. See you tonight."

After he ended the call, he realized he couldn't go on this way. Leslie needed reassurance, but Sadie's unexpected return to Montana had altered the path he'd been plodding since she'd left, throwing him into the greatest turmoil of his life.

What Daniel had told her that night had crystalized certain things for Jarod. If the statute of limitations hadn't run out and he could discover the proof, Ned would be facing felony assault charges for using a borrowed truck as a deadly weapon. Worse, because he'd left the scene of the crime without reporting it or getting help for Jarod, Ned would be looking at prison time.

If he didn't reopen the case, the most Jarod would do was go to Tyson and Grant with any evidence he found and let them deal with Ned in their own way.

His hand tightened around the phone, almost crushing it. What if he did find enough evidence to have the case reopened?

If Jarod's uncle Charlo knew what was going through his nephew's mind right now, he would intimate that the reason Jarod hadn't received his vision yet was because his cry was selfish. Only those who were of exemplary character and well prepared received the truly great visions. With the taste for revenge this strong on Jarod's lips, he was far from that serene place his uncle talked about.

Chapter 5

Saturday morning Sadie got breakfast for her and Ryan and then they went outside to an overcast sky. The small garden plot on the south wall of the house where it received the most sun needed work. While she watched Ryan toddle around with some toys, Sadie prepared the soil, then laid out black plastic to warm it up, a trick she'd learned from Addie Bannock years earlier. In a week she'd plant seeds.

While her mouth salivated at the thought of enjoying sweet juicy melons all summer, her cell phone rang. She wished it were Jarod, yet she knew that was impossible. As Millie had said, Sadie needed to be the one to tell him there was no other man in her life. But that was complicated because he was seeing another woman.

Even if he wanted to call Sadie, which he didn't, he would have to use the landline because he didn't know her cell phone number. With a troubled sigh she pulled the cell from her pocket and checked the Caller ID. One glance and her spirits lifted.

"Zane! How are things going?"

"Couldn't be better. I've had all our mail forwarded to White Lodge. Right now I'm at the house sorting things. Tomorrow the moving van will come to put everything in storage. When they're through here, they'll load up the things from my apartment. How's Ryan?"

"Missing you. Just a minute. He'll want to talk to you." She walked over to her brother. "Ryan? It's your uncle Zane. Can you say hello?"

After Ryan greeted his uncle and babbled some other words not quite intelligible, she heard Zane chuckle and a conversation ensued with Ryan mentioning the juice he'd had for breakfast and one of the toy cars he held in his hand.

"You have to hang up now," she told the little boy. "Tell Uncle Zane bye-bye."

Ryan liked saying the words over and over, but finally Sadie put the phone back to her ear. "If I do the planting right, we'll have fresh honeydew all summer."

"How about some cantaloupe, too!"

"I'll plant some of those and maybe some green beans."

"Terrific. Have you heard from Mr. Bree yet?"

"No. I don't really expect to until you have a prospective buyer for Tim's house."

"Let's hope it's soon, but at least our Realtor has contacted him and knows we're serious. If all goes well here, I'll have the cleaners come and leave for Billings sometime Sunday in my Volvo. It can hold the main stuff you wanted me to bring along with my own."

"That's great. What about my Toyota?"

"The salesman at the dealership said he'd get a good price for it."

"I hope so. Dad's old truck is on its last legs. I need to buy a used one."

"Understood. Depending on how late I get

away, it might be Monday night before I reach the ranch."

"We'll be waiting. Ryan will be thrilled. He keeps looking for you." Right now he was down on his haunches, pushing his little trucks and cars through the grass.

"I can't believe how much I've missed him." Her throat swelled. "He's adorable."

"Amen."

"Is it going to be difficult to pull up stakes, Zane?"

"No. I'll always have my good memories, but my life isn't here anymore."

"I know what you mean. Much as I love San Francisco, my home is here."

After a silence, Zane told her, "Don't work too hard, Sadie."

"It's saving my life." Along with making a new home for Ryan, she needed to stay too busy to think. She'd tackled cleaning the house, including her father's bedroom. Now the outside needed attention. "Thank you for taking care of everything, Zane. I don't know what I'd do without you."

"We're family. Let's agree we both need each other. Because of you I can feel a whole new life opening up. When everything fell apart, I couldn't imagine putting one foot in front of the other."

She cleared her throat. "I've been there and done that."

"I know you have." He knew the secrets of her heart. "Talk to you soon."

"Drive safely, Zane." Her voice trembled. "If anything happened to you…"

"It won't."

As Sadie hung up, she felt a shadow fall over her. When she lifted her head she discovered Jarod standing there.

"Sorry," he said in his deep voice. "Once again I've startled you. Millie was out on the front porch washing windows and told me to walk around back."

After wishing he'd been the one who'd phoned her, she was so shocked to see him, she couldn't think clearly. Somehow on Jarod a denim shirt and jeans looked spectacular. "No problem. As you can see, I've been getting the ground ready to plant."

"Shades of my grandmother Addie."

She nodded. He remembered everything.

His enigmatic black eyes swept over her. "I drove over here to talk to you about the accident."

Jarod's reason for coming was as unexpected as his presence. Sadie struggled to keep the tremor out of her voice. "Since you didn't believe me about my father, I'm afraid any answers you need are buried with him."

He put his hands on his hips; pulling her attention to his hard-muscled physique. "I've given it a lot of thought and I don't believe your father was the culprit, Sadie. That's why I'm here."

Shock number two. "But he said—"

"What he did was use a scare tactic to frighten you away from me for good," Jarod cut in on her. "I'm convinced that when he heard I was in the hospital, he realized it was the perfect moment to play on your fears."

Sadie was afraid to believe it. "Then who could have done such an evil thing?" She removed her gardening gloves.

"I've been doing an investigation and hope to figure it out before long. I wanted you to know that no matter how much pain your father caused you, he wasn't responsible for trying to hurt me or he would have done it much earlier. Though he wished I hadn't been in your life, we both know he was a troubled man with a terrible drinking problem. But it didn't go as far as planning to kill me, so you can cross him off your list."

Her lungs had constricted, making it difficult to breathe. "But according to you, someone *did* want you dead."

His eyes narrowed on her features. "The police and I both felt that the accident had to have been premeditated. Someone went to elaborate lengths to set me up. It took someone whose dislike of me turned to hate. I'll give you one guess."

Suddenly she felt sick. *"Ned,"* she whispered.

"I'm afraid so."

"After you told me he'd been stalking you in town, I thought a lot about that myself. But for him to go after you like that…"

"It chills the blood to think he could have done it to his own family, but I can't rule him out as the prime suspect."

"I agree," she whispered. Being a year younger than Jarod, Ned had been a senior when she'd started high school. He'd always chased after her. The more she'd ignored him, the more he'd mocked her friendship with his "half-breed cousin."

"He never hid his dislike of you."

After his graduation Ned had hung out in White Lodge with his friends and followed her around whenever she went into town. His actions were repulsive to her.

"You're the one girl who never gave him the time of day, but he never stopped wanting you. As our love grew, so did his jealousy. It's my belief he'd been following me on those last few nights when we met in the mountains. But I didn't realize it until the night before you and I were going to leave for the reservation. I caught him spying on me as I rode to the barn."

Horrified, Sadie stared at him. "You think he was watching us wh-when—" She couldn't finish.

"That's exactly what I think. But he couldn't go to my grandfather claiming to have seen us when he had no reason to be watching us. That would have opened up a whole new set of problems for him."

"He was sick!"

Jarod nodded. "The next afternoon after I hitched the horse trailer to my truck, he saw me leave with Chief and knew I was getting ready to do something with you. So he set me up, but he needed an accomplice and couldn't use one of our trucks on the ranch."

"Who would help him do anything that hideous?"

"His best friend, Owen."

"Owen Pearson? Cindy's brother?" She was incredulous. "I know they used to drink and mess around like a lot of guys, but I can't imagine him doing anything like that."

"I found out from my grandfather that Ned and Owen committed a crime a few years ago but it was hushed up." Jarod told her what he'd learned from Harlow. "Ned could wheedle money from his father when he wanted. Don't forget he and Owen have been friends for years and got into so much trouble, Ralph claims it turned Grant prematurely gray."

"I didn't realize Ned gave your family that many worries. It's still hard for me to believe Owen would go that far."

"I've been doing my own investigation." Jarod reached in his back pocket and handed her a sheet of paper, which she opened. It was a photocopy of a receipt from a body shop in Bozeman. The repairs listed included grill and front fender work on a 2003 Ford F-150 pickup owned by Kevin Pearson of the Bar-S Ranch, brought in on May 10 and repairs completed May 16 of the year in question.

"Jarod—" She lifted her eyes to him. Streams of unspoken words passed between them.

"The manager of the shop didn't recognize Ned's picture. It's been too many years. But whoever took the truck in paid cash up front. I checked the police report on my truck, which was totaled. Once I contact the department that investigated my case and give them this receipt, then the case will be reopened to see if there's a match between the two vehicles."

"That means they'll be contacting the Pearsons about the truck." Sadie frowned. "What if it has been sold or traded in for another one by now?"

"The police will track it down. Owen will have to fess up to what happened to his father's truck. Unless, of course, it's a huge coincidence and his father's truck was damaged some other way. But if that was the case, why didn't he let the insurance pay for it?

"I'm afraid he has a lot of explaining to do. If he was helping Ned, then he'll have to make the decision if he wants to go to jail for him or not. But I'm not ready to act quite yet."

Sadie's eyes stung with salty tears. "I don't know why you have to wait. This couldn't be a coincidence. Ned could have killed you— All this time I thought it was my father." Her body grew tense. "Your cousin should go to prison for what he did. You were left to die—"

Her raised voice alarmed Ryan, who stood and came running to her with an anxious look on his precious face. She swept him up into her arms and buried her face in his neck.

"But I didn't," Jarod said in a quiet voice, tousling Ryan's hair. "I'm pretty sure he didn't intend to finish me off, just put me out of commission. As for his plan, it backfired because I was back on the ranch three days later and you'd fled to California out of his reach. Your departure put an end to any dreams Ned entertained about the two of you getting together."

"He was delusional."

"I agree. But now that you're back, he's going to make trouble again."

Her stomach muscles clenched. "What do you mean?"

"I know for a fact he hasn't given up on you. Avery told me about the incident at the funeral when Ned approached you. Be careful around him."

That sounded ominous. "What aren't you telling me?"

"I suppose we'll all find out when this new investigation gets under way. I'll leave now so you can give your little brother the attention he's craving. He really looks like his uncle."

"It's the dimples. They run in the Lawson family. Mom fell in love with Tim's. It kills me Ryan has been deprived of both parents."

"He has a wonderful mother in you."

"Thank you. I'm planning to adopt him."

"Then he's a lucky little boy. Take care, Sadie, and remember what I said."

"Jarod? Wait—" she called to him, but he moved too fast on those long, powerful legs. She couldn't very well run after him with Ryan in her arms. Her brother needed lunch and a nap.

Sadie hurried inside, shaken by everything he'd told her and even more shaken by the things he'd only hinted at. Millie stood at the kitchen sink filling another bucket with hot water and vinegar. "Jarod was here a long time. Everything all right?"

"Yes and no." She didn't dare share the

evidence Jarod had uncovered until he gave her permission. But one thing had become self-evident. Her longing to be with him was growing unbearable.

Millie started out the back door, then paused. Sadie thought she detected a faint smile on the older woman's lips. "After you've fed Ryan and put him down, come on outside where I'm working. There's something you ought to know."

With one of those cryptic comments Millie was famous for, Sadie hurried to feed Ryan and put him down with a bottle. The cute little guy had tired himself out playing and fell asleep fast.

She found Millie washing the windows at the rear of the house. "I'm back."

The housekeeper looked over her shoulder at Sadie. "When Jarod drove in, he was pulling a horse trailer. After he left, I saw him drive to the barn and pull around it. Kind of made me wonder what he was doing when the road back to his place goes in the other direction. If I were you, I'd walk down there and find out what's going on."

Sadie's heart raced till it hurt. Feeling seventeen again, she flew down the drive past her father's truck to the barn. But when she rounded the corner, Jarod's rig wasn't there and her heart plummeted to her feet.

After hearing her call to him, had he hoped she'd come after him? Until she had answers, she wouldn't be able to breathe. While she stood there in a quandary, she heard Liz's horses whinnying and wondered what was going on.

She opened the barn doors. "Hey, you guys. What's up?" She walked inside to check both stalls. All of a sudden she heard the neigh of another horse. It couldn't be Mac's. He was out working on his horse, Toby.

Sadie spun around. The light from outside illuminated the interior enough for her to see a gleaming black filly in the stall where she'd once kept Brandy. Her body started to tremble as she moved closer to the three-year-old, which looked to be fourteen hands high.

This couldn't be the foal she'd seen in the purple lupine with Jarod when she was seventeen! That wasn't possible, but the filly had those special hooked ears and broad forehead that tapered to the muzzle, just the way Sadie remembered. On further examination she saw the straight head and wide-set eyes of Chief, the wild stallion Jarod had tamed.

"Oh, you gorgeous creature," she whispered shakily. Sadie didn't need to ask where this beauty had come from. "I'll be back, but first I need to know all about you before this goes any further. I promise I won't be long."

Sadie's feet seemed to have wings as she flew up the road to the house. "Millie?"

The housekeeper turned around. "I'm right here!"

"I've got to find Jarod. Do you mind watching Ryan until I get back?"

"Of course not, honey. What's going on?"

Sadie ran in the house to grab the keys off the peg. When she came out she said, "There's a new filly in the barn. I can't keep her. Jarod needs to come back and get it."

Before she reached the truck a voice of irony called out, "Good luck to that."

Five minutes later she drove through the gates of the Bannock Ranch. The spread resembled a small city. She took the road leading to the barn and corrals where Jarod would have parked the horse trailer. Intent on finding him, she wound around the sheds until she saw his rig in the distance. He still hadn't unhitched the trailer.

After pulling up next to it, she jumped down from the truck. As she reached the entrance, the man she'd come to see was just leaving the barn on his horse. Riding bareback, the magnificent sight of him ready to head out took her breath. His long black hair, fastened at the nape, gleamed despite the gathering storm clouds blotting out the sun.

They saw each other at the same time. He was caught off guard for once, and his eyes gleamed black fire as they roved over her, thrilling her to the core of her being. While she stood there out of breath, he brought his horse close before coming to a standstill.

She couldn't swallow. "I have to talk to you, Jarod."

How she envied him sitting there as still as a summer's day. "I'm going to ride to the upper pasture. Come with me."

Before she could respond, he reached down with that swift male grace only he possessed and lifted her so she was seated in front of him. He wrapped his left arm around her waist and tucked her up tight against him.

The way his hand splayed over her midriff infused electricity in every cell of her body.

"Reminds me of old times," he murmured against her temple, "except this time I'll be able to see where we're going. Don't get me wrong. I like your new hairstyle, but now I don't have anything to tug."

That rare teasing side of Jarod had come out, the side she adored. Robbed of words, she was helpless to do anything but give in to the euphoria of being this close to him again. Though it had been eight years, their bodies knew each other and settled in as one entity.

Once he urged his horse into a gallop, the layers of pain peeled away, liberating her for a moment out of time. Heedless of the darkening clouds, they were like children who'd been let out of school and were eager to run until they dropped.

She quickly lost track of where they were going. This was like flying through heaven, achieving heights and distant stars unknown until now. Filled with delight, she heard laughter and realized it was her own. Through it all her body absorbed the fierce pounding of his heart against her back.

At one point it dawned on her he'd brought

them to the pine-covered ridge that looked down on their favorite place. He reined his horse to a stop so they could enjoy the meadow with its vista of wildflowers in glorious bloom.

She gripped the hand pinning her against him. *"Jarod..."*

"I haven't heard you say my name like that except in my sleep. Did you ever dream of me?"

This was a time for honesty.

"Yes," she admitted quietly.

"Every night?"

Haunted by the agony she heard in his voice because it matched her own, she said, "Don't ask me that. It's all in the past. I came to find you because—"

"The filly is yours, Sadie." The authority in his voice signaled the end of the discussion. "Now that the war is over, consider it a peace offering."

She was still in shock over his incredible gift, but it was growing darker. "Jarod, we'd better go back before we get caught in the rain."

"It's too late. We'll stay in the shelter of

these pines until it passes over. Volan needs a rest."

He slid off his horse in an instant and gripped her waist to help her down. After tying the reins to a tree branch, he walked her over to the fattest tree trunk and sat against it, pulling her onto his lap. By now the wind was gusting, bringing the smell of rain with it.

"This is only a small storm. We'll wait it out." He gathered her to him in a protective gesture. Cocooned in his warmth, she could stay like this forever. "If you're worried about getting wet, I promise I'll protect you."

She relaxed against him. "Tell me about the adorable filly."

"Chief was her sire."

"I *knew* it. She has the shape of his head and eyes."

"It took two tries with the black broodmare I acquired to produce her." She could tell by the softness in his voice that her observation had pleased him. "Her first offspring was a grullo I gave to Uncle Charlo's boy."

"You mean, Squealing Son Who Runs Fast?"

Jarod chuckled. "You remember."

"I remember everything," she confessed in

a tremulous voice. "He must be fifteen by now."

"The perfect age to train his own stallion. But that was his childhood name. Now he's known as Runs Over Mountains."

"Sounds like he has some of the same genes that run through his noble cousin Sits in the Center."

He kissed the side of her brow, sending fingers of delight through her nervous system. "What happened to Born of Flint?"

Jarod had forgiven her. "That name belonged to my world when pain was my constant companion. But seriously, Jarod, no gift has ever thrilled me more. I love her already."

"Your filly has been registered as Black Velvet. Until now, she has lived at the reservation on my uncle's property. I've been getting her used to a saddle, but you'll need to break her in more before you take her riding."

Sadie gripped his hand harder. Velvet was the name she'd given the new foal they'd seen that wonderful day years ago. Now Sadie had her own filly, a horse who'd known nothing but Jarod's love. She had to clear her throat. "Velvet has been trained by the expert. Thank you doesn't begin to cover what I'm feeling, not when I've done nothing to deserve such a present."

"When my grandfather told me you were going to stay in Montana, I realized you would need a horse."

"Your uncle Charlo must be bursting with pride."

"What do you mean?"

"Do you remember the time you took me to meet him and his family? Before we left he took me aside and told me you possessed a very rare trait like your mother. It was the ability to hear the cries of the oppressed, the sick, the weak. He said that you weren't ashamed to help others.

"I didn't understand what he meant at the time, but I do now. After I visited Ralph last week he told you everything about my situation, didn't he?"

Before she heard his answer, the rain descended, first in individual drops, then it poured, yet they stayed dry. She nestled deeper in his arms, finding a comfort she'd never known in her life, except with him. Together they listened to the elements that had always made up their world.

His lips were buried in her hair. "You think I see you as a charity case?"

"I think that's the way you've always seen me. A cast-off waif you took pity on because it's in your nature. After eight years, you're still coming to my rescue, trying to right wrongs against me by giving me Velvet. I'll be indebted to you all my life for everything you've done for me in the past, but it's time you gave that side of your nature a rest in order to walk your true path."

He lifted his head in surprise. "My true path?"

"Mmm." The downpour was easing in intensity. She moved out of his arms and stood. "The one you used to talk about that will lead to your ultimate destiny."

After a long silence he asked, "What about yours?"

"Mine was revealed when my mother died and left Ryan to my care."

Before she gave in to her longing and begged him to kiss her, she needed answers about the woman who was in his life now. "Tell me about Leslie Weston."

Immediately he got to his feet. "Listening

to so many wagging tongues tends to confuse the listener."

"If you're talking about the way you were confused with wagging tongues concerning me and Zane at the funeral, you're right. But please don't be offended. I've heard she's a lovely woman who works with Avery at the dig site. Your grandfather sounded particularly taken with her, which means you're on the right path."

"Grandfathers are prone to dream."

"Liz tells me that not only is Leslie a highly educated archaeologist studying the Crow culture, she's also well-traveled and comes from a good family in Colorado Springs. How important is she to you?"

"Why do you ask?" His tone grated.

Don't tiptoe around this, Sadie. "Because when word gets out where Velvet came from, I don't want her to misunderstand or be hurt."

After the telltale rise and fall of his chest, he said, "The rain has stopped. We need to get back to the ranch."

Instead of a protestation that the woman he'd been involved with meant nothing to him, he was ready to leave this sacred place. Sadie had her answer. She just hadn't expected it to feel as if one of those wild stallions they used to watch had just kicked her in the chest, knocking the life out of her.

Schooling her features to show no emotion, she turned to him. "This time I'll sit behind you. That way I can tug on *your* hair for a change."

Her teasing produced no softening of his stone-faced expression. As he walked over to Volan, she followed him. "I liked the way you used to wear it, but I'm glad you gave in to the right impulse to let it grow.

"I know you'll hate hearing this because you don't like compliments, but now that I'm grown up, I'm not afraid to say what I think. You're a very beautiful man, Sits in the Center. Leslie Weston would have figured that out the first time she laid eyes on you."

In seconds he'd vaulted onto Volan's back with practiced ease, then held out his hand for Sadie to climb on behind him. She settled herself and slid her arms around his waist. If she couldn't kiss the life out of him because he belonged to someone else, she could at least hold him in her arms for the ride home.

Judging from his reaction to her question about Leslie, this would be the only time she would ever be allowed to get this close to him again. As the rain that had cleared the air, this conversation had cleared away the last piece in the complicated mosaic of their lives. Their love story had come to its final, tragic close.

Chapter 6

Jarod's uncle Charlo knew of his nephew's struggle to let Leslie or any woman into his life while another woman lived in his heart. This Saturday afternoon Sadie's question ended the struggle. He knew what had to be done to end a situation that couldn't go on any longer.

As they rode back to Jarod's ranch in silence, his uncle's analogy about the wolf took on fresh meaning. It *would* be better to risk death for a chance to find a mate and a territory than to live through every winter in agony alone.

Weighed down by his thoughts, he was surprised to hear Sadie's sudden gasp as they approached the barn. He glanced over to see what had caused the reaction. If it wasn't Ned coming out of the barn on foot! Once again it was no accident he'd been hanging around. He must have seen Daniel Corkin's truck and put two and two together. Jarod thought his cousin looked a little green around the edges. Wasn't that jealousy's color?

Sadie's arms tightened around Jarod as he rode his horse straight to her truck. Aware of her fear, he threw his leg over Volan and pulled her off, then opened the driver's door. "In you go," he whispered, shutting it after her.

Their eyes met for a breathless moment before she started the engine and took off. He stood there watching until she'd driven out of sight.

Ned smirked at him. "Leslie's not going to like it when she finds out what you've been doing all afternoon."

Jarod turned to look at his cousin. "I'm afraid there's a lot more you're not going to like when your father hears you've been spending time in town minding other people's business rather than inspecting the machinery."

When Jarod had hired Ben as the new foreman, one of his jobs was to keep a close eye on Ned, who was lax in his responsibilities and played hooky when he thought he could get away with it. Ben reported Ned's activities to Jarod on a daily basis. Ned's assigned job was to keep all the ranch machinery in good condition and operational, but he often failed in that department, which added to Jarod's workload.

"What in the hell are you talking about?"

"The grain-cutting swathers and forage harvesters for one thing. They haven't been oiled or greased on time. That's your department. One of the grain trucks has a broken part that needs replacing. Have you taken a look at the Haybine mowers lately? If I were you, I'd get busy or it could all rebound on you."

Ned's cheeks turned a ruddy color, a sure sign of guilt. "What do you mean?"

"That's for *you* to figure out." From the corner of his eye, he glimpsed Rusty, the stable manager, and signaled to him. "We got caught in the storm, and now I'm in a hurry. Will you take care of Volan for me? He'll need a rubdown."

"Sure, Jarod."

Ignoring Ned, Jarod walked over to his rig to unhitch the trailer. The puddles from the cloudburst were still drifting away. Climbing into his truck, he drove out of the parking area without acknowledging his cousin and headed for White Lodge.

Leslie would be off work by now. He hoped to find her at her apartment. He knew she'd sensed something was wrong on their dinner date Wednesday. It was time they talked. She lived in an eight-plex near the center of town where they usually met before going out for the evening. He'd brought her out to the ranch one time to meet his grandfather, but it was easier for them to get together in White Lodge, the halfway point between her work and the ranch.

Both his grandfather and uncle approved of her. Charlo had been amenable to her interviewing him for a newsletter she contributed to about the Absarokee dig site. There was nothing not to like about Leslie. But she wasn't Sadie.

Pleased to see her Forerunner parked in her

stall, he drove to the guest parking and got out of his truck. Taking the stairs two at a time, he reached her apartment and gave a knock she would recognize.

He didn't have to wait long for her to open the door. "Jarod—" She broke into a smile that lit up her brown eyes. "I didn't know you were coming tonight. Why didn't you say something at dinner the other night or phone me?"

"I'm sorry I didn't give you any warning, but this couldn't wait."

When he didn't reach to kiss her, her smile slowly disappeared. "Come in. Is this about your grandfather? Is he worse?"

He walked into her living room. "No. I'm happy to say he's doing better and off his oxygen for the time being."

"That's wonderful! Have you eaten yet? I just made homemade fajitas. Would you like one?"

"They smell good, but I'm not hungry. Go ahead and eat." He took a seat in one of her overstuffed chairs.

She frowned. "I don't think I can till you tell me what's wrong. You're not yourself. In fact, for the past two weeks you haven't been the Jarod I've known."

He shook his head. "I realize that."

Leslie perched on the arm of the sofa, studying him. "You wouldn't have come here out of the blue like this without a good reason. Have you decided you don't want to see me anymore?" He heard the pain in her voice.

Jarod met her searching gaze head-on. "I can't," he answered. She deserved the whole truth no matter how much it hurt. He was glad he hadn't been intimate with her yet.

Her features looked pinched. "Avery hinted that there was someone in your past. Are you saying you can't get over her?"

He got to his feet. "I thought I'd put her behind me, but her father died and now she's back in Montana for good. I was with her today."

She averted her eyes. "And the old chemistry is still working."

The blood hammered in his ears. "Yes. Don't get me wrong. We're not together. I don't know if we ever will be, but feeling as I do—"

"I get it," she broke in. "Do you mind my asking who she is?"

"Her name is Sadie Corkin. The Corkin ranch borders our property."

Leslie stood. "Childhood sweethearts?"

"Yes."

"That's an obstacle I'm not even going to attempt to hurdle. One of the many things I admire about you, Jarod, is your honesty, even when it's devastating."

"Leslie… I was trying to make it work with us."

She walked over to the door, her curly auburn hair swinging slightly. "I believe you and I give you full marks, but in the end, trying doesn't cut it. That explains why you weren't anxious to sleep with me, or to drive to Colorado with me."

"If she'd never come back, things might have been different."

"No." Leslie shook her head. "If she hadn't come back, our relationship would still have ended because it's evident you're a one-woman man. There aren't very many of those around." She clung to the open door. "I've loved every minute we've spent together."

"So have I."

"Because of who you are, I know you mean that."

"I do."

"But it's just not enough for me or you.

Love means sharing a single soul inhabiting two bodies. That definition doesn't apply to you and me. I'm grateful you stopped by, Jarod, but now I need to be alone."

Jarod had no desire to make this any more painful. "Take care, Leslie." He kissed her forehead before leaving the apartment. He wished there was some way he could have spared her this hurt. No one deserved happiness more than she did.

On his drive back to the ranch, her parting comment played over in his mind. He and Sadie *had* shared one soul. That's why no other relationship had worked for him. But he still didn't know about the men she'd been involved with since she'd moved to California.

If there was someone important, she wasn't letting it get in the way of buying the ranch and living here. So many questions still remained unanswered where Sadie was concerned. But saying goodbye to Leslie had been the right thing to do.

When he entered the front door of the ranch house, the housekeeper came running. "I'm glad you're home. Your grandfather is in an agitated state."

He moaned. "I thought the doctor had taken him off the oxygen."

She shook her head. "It's not his health, Jarod. Tyson was here earlier and they quarreled." *Tyson?* "He's terribly upset about something and says he can't discuss it with anyone but you."

Jarod's gut told him this had to be about Ned, especially after their confrontation earlier. "Where's Avery?"

"She's not home yet."

"Thanks, Jenny." He hurried down the hall to his grandfather's bedroom and found him sitting up at his desk near the window in his pajamas and robe. Though he was gratified to see Ralph was well enough to be out of bed, Jenny's mention of Tyson had filled him with concern.

"Grandfather?"

He looked around with a flushed face. "At last."

"What's happened?"

"What hasn't?" he said with uncharacteristic sharpness. "I'm sorry, son. I didn't mean to snap. I'm just glad you're home. Sit down. We have to talk."

Jarod pulled up a chair next to the desk. "I can see you've been going over the accounts."

Ralph's gray eyes flicked to his. "Tyson needed me to help him with the figures. He just left. I'm afraid we had it out. It's been coming on for a long time. After our father died, Addie warned me I should let my brother take his share of the ranch and make it his own place. But he begged me to go into business with him and I didn't have the heart to say no. For the most part we've gotten along. But with time, there've been issues over Ned. He doesn't have your instincts for ranching and never did.

"Your idea of developing two calving seasons a few years ago has brought in unprecedented profits. When Tyson and I went along with your plan, Ned fell apart and has been impossible ever since. Now that Ned has found out the Corkin property is up for sale, he's asked for a loan from Grant to buy it."

Jarod got up from the chair and started pacing. "Let me guess. Grant's money is stretched due to helping his other children, so he's come to Tyson for $700,000 for Ned to buy the place."

Ralph nodded. "Grant's always been afraid

of Ned and doesn't know how to say no to him. It's Grant's opinion that if Ned made a break with the family business and had his own spread to manage, his son might turn into a real rancher."

"We know that's never going to happen."

His grandfather shook his head. "I advised Tyson it would be the wrong decision to give money to a grandson who could never make good on such an investment. But just as I feared, he got angry. My brother isn't well and not up for a fight with Grant. He told me he'd be back tomorrow for my consent. If I don't give it, he'll take the money out, any-way. Of course, it's his right as part owner."

They stared at each other before Jarod said, "What do you want to do? Tell Tyson you've already authorized Harlow to buy the ranch for Sadie and Zane?"

"Never. That has to remain a secret."

Jarod didn't need to think about it. "Then don't try to stop him, Grandfather. You love your brother too much, so make your peace with him and let him negotiate with Mr. Bree. When the time is almost up, Harlow will come in with a little higher offer and that will be it.

"In time Tyson and Grant will learn that

Zane Lawson bought the ranch and no one will ever know the truth because the money came out of your savings account and mine. Tyson has no access to them."

His grandfather tilted his head back. "What do you mean *your* account?"

"I've been investing my money and plan to contribute. Sadie'd be my wife if things had been different."

"I know." Ralph's eyes dimmed. "When Addie and I heard about your accident, it was one of the worst moments of our lives. We could have lost you." His voice trembled.

Touched by those words, Jarod squeezed his shoulder. "Don't you know I'm tough like you? Now that you're feeling better, I have news. Let me show you what I found after doing some investigating about the accident on my own."

Jarod showed his grandfather the paper from the body shop in Bozeman incriminating Owen Pearson.

Tears rolled down Ralph's cheeks. "Oh, Jarod… All these years I've asked you to be the bigger man, which you always will be. To think Ned could have done such a thing. It explains why his behavior has grown worse over time. You have every right to go to the police with what you've found."

"That's true." For now he was holding off deciding what to do about it. "Did Sadie tell you she's going to adopt Ryan?"

"Yes, bless her heart." His grandfather reached for Jarod's hand. "Now tell me about that lovely woman you brought to the house a while back. When are you going to bring her again?"

"I'm afraid that's not going to happen, Grandfather."

"Why not?"

"I drove to White Lodge earlier this evening and told Leslie the truth. I can't be involved with her while I still have feelings for Sadie."

"You've done the right thing for Leslie and yourself," he murmured with what sounded like satisfaction. "A house divided against itself can't stand."

In spite of his turmoil, Jarod smiled. He bounced between two cultures. Both his mentors offered the same wisdom.

"So." His grandfather sat back in the chair looking relieved. "We'll keep all this to ourselves and wait a few more days before we tell

Harlow to make the final move. When everything has been transacted, Harlow can contact Zane and they'll go from there."

Jarod's thoughts shot ahead. "It's good it will be in Zane's name." He gave his grandfather a hug. "I'll tell Martha to come in and help you get ready for bed."

Ralph tugged on his arm. "Do me a favor, son. Watch your back around Ned. I need you."

The feeling was mutual.

Ryan was ecstatic when Zane came into the kitchen on Tuesday morning. He'd arrived late Monday night. While the two of them walked down to the barn to visit the new filly Sadie had told him about, she had hurriedly put the things away that Zane had brought from California. Now Ryan had his toys and pictures, and his room resembled the nursery Eileen had made for him in San Francisco.

After lunch he went down for a nap with his favorite furry rabbit.

Zane was bringing in the last of his own items from the car when Sadie stepped out onto the front porch dressed in cowboy boots, jeans and a short-sleeved white blouse. She'd tied an old black paisley bandana around her neck for fun.

"You look cute in that."

"Thanks. When I saw it in the sack you brought in, it brought back memories. I thought, why not look the part."

"All you need is a cowboy hat."

She smiled. "I'm afraid my old one got lost years ago. While Ryan's asleep, I'll run into town and pick one up when I get the groceries."

"Take as long as you want. I plan to devote the rest of the day to him once he wakes up."

"He'll love that. We're so glad you're back safely."

"Me, too." His eyes glinted with curiosity. "That horse is a beauty. For Jarod to give you a present like that means he still cares for you a great deal."

She shook her head. "He feels sorry for me."

"Sadie—"

"It's true. He knew Dad sold my old horse. Before you say anything else, you need to know Jarod's involved with another woman and it's serious."

Zane frowned. "Did he tell you that?"

It was more a case of his not answering her question about Leslie Weston when they'd been out riding the other day. "I've heard it from his grandfather and from Liz, who's very close with Avery. Now, I'd better get going. See you later and we'll talk."

They only had two weeks left to work out an arrangement with Mr. Bree. So far she'd been living on some of her savings while they'd pooled their resources. With the days passing so quickly, Sadie's fear escalated that their best efforts might not be enough. But she refused to think about that yet, or the possibility that Jarod might be getting married in the near future. Millie had sounded as though she thought it could happen.

After loading up on groceries in White Lodge, Sadie put the bags in the truck, then decided to buy herself a treat in the hope it would make her feel better. The Saddle Up Barn was just down the street. She'd drop by there for a cowboy hat.

It didn't take her long to find the one she wanted. Black, like her new filly, like... Jarod's eyes and hair. The band and sides of the brim were covered in a delicate gold floral pattern that picked up the gold-and-silver cowboy concho on the band. She was partial to the pinch-front, teardrop crown that gave it character.

After paying the bill, she walked out of the shop wearing the hat and was met by a barrage of wolf whistles from various guys passing by in their rigs. Their response reminded her of her barrel racing days in her teens. She'd almost forgotten what that experience was like.

Every time she and Liz performed at the county rodeo she'd watch for Jarod, hoping he'd be in the crowd with his family to cheer on Connor, who was a fabulous bulldogger. Being a contestant, she often carried the Montana State flag as they paraded around the arena for the opening ceremony. During those times when she was all decked out in her hat and fancy Western shirt with the fringe, she'd feel Jarod's piercing black eyes staring at her and almost faint with excitement.

The memories swamped her, causing her to forget she was headed for the post office. She needed to mail the thank-you notes she'd written to all the people who'd sent flowers for the funeral. While she was buying a book of stamps from the machine, she heard her name called out in a familiar voice and turned around.

"Avery!" Her heart raced to see Jarod's sister come up to her, a smile lighting her gray-green eyes. Avery and Jarod shared similar facial features that identified them as Bannocks.

"I've been following you since I saw you walking across the street. Do you know you caused about a dozen accidents out there?" Sadie laughed in embarrassment. "It's true. You used to knock them dead at the rodeo, but your impact is more lethal now."

"It's the new hat."

"That's bull and you know it. In high school the guys voted you Queen of Montana Days your senior year. To get that nomination, let alone win, you had to be able to stop traffic for *all* the right reasons."

"Stop—" She gave her friend a hug. Avery could make her blush.

"I'm glad I ran into you. Since Connor will be home, we're going to throw a surprise family birthday party on Monday the twenty-ninth, for Grandpa, who's going to be eighty-four. He's feeling so well we thought it would be fun to invite a few close friends.

Our cousin Cassie will be coming from Great Falls, of course, and can't wait to see you. Naturally everyone on the Farfields Ranch is invited, including the Hensons, Ryan's uncle Zane and that cute little brother of yours."

Sadie could hardly breathe. It would mean facing Jarod, who would be there with Leslie Weston. Maybe they were celebrating more than a birthday. She felt ill at the possibility, but she'd have to go even if it killed her.

"Sadie, don't worry about Ned," Avery added. "Connor has orders to keep him away from you."

"Thanks." But Ned had been the furthest thing from her mind. "We'd love to come." Sadie marveled that she was even able to get the words out. "I'll tell Millie as soon as I get back to the ranch."

"Wonderful. It'll be very low key. Please, no gifts. I'm making his favorite homemade hand-cranked pineapple ice cream, Grandma Myra's recipe. When he sees what I'm doing, he'll want to help me."

"Don't let him do it, Avery!"

She chuckled. "Try telling him that. Come any time after six-thirty. Grandpa gets tired fast and goes to bed early."

"We'll be there. What can I bring?"

"Yourselves!"

Sadie gave her another hug. When Jarod had asked her to marry him, she'd been so thrilled that Avery was going to be her sister-in-law. Instead, Leslie Weston would be the luckiest woman on earth to become a part of that family.

"See you then, Avery." She watched her leave, then put the stamps on the envelopes and mailed them. With her heart dragging on the sidewalk, she headed back to the truck. How in the name of heaven would she get through the party when she knew Jarod would be there?

Maybe at the last minute she could claim Ryan was running a temperature. Zane could go without her. She'd send Ralph her apologies in a written note. Zane would deliver it with her gift and tell him she'd be over when Ryan was better. She and Ralph would celebrate with a card game.

On impulse she drove to Chapman's Drugstore and bought him two packs of playing cards and a card shuffler with new batteries. She also bought some wrapping paper and a silly birthday card Ralph would understand with his sense of humor. It said, "Grandfather still looks pretty good on his birthday. If it just hadn't been for_____." You could fill the line in with anything you wanted.

Without having to think about it Sadie wrote "the neighbors."

Chapter 7

Avery had coordinated their grandfather's birthday party with Jarod and Connor's help. She'd hired caterers to do the cooking and serving out on the back patio. Jarod couldn't have been happier when he'd learned she'd included Sadie and the Hensons in the guest list.

Because of Ned, Jarod's afternoon ride with Sadie had ended abruptly, leaving things hanging. Since then he'd broken it off with Leslie, but due to the long hours of calving season, this would be Jarod's first opportunity to get Sadie alone and answer the question of Leslie's importance in his life.

The evening of the party, after a shower and shave, he put on a silky black sport shirt and gray trousers. This was a special occasion. Six weeks ago his grandfather had been in the hospital and Jarod had feared he wouldn't come out again. But he'd rallied and in some respects seemed better than he had been in several months. Jarod was convinced Sadie's presence on the Corkin ranch had had a lot to do with the change in him.

Ralph was furious over Daniel's shameless treatment of her. To help her keep the ranch in her family was a gesture that revealed the depth of his affection for her. Like Jarod, he was in this fight to win. The end of the month couldn't come soon enough for either of them. After Harlow bought the ranch, they could all breathe more easily again.

Once he was ready, he went downstairs. "You look distinguished in that new gray suit, Grandfather. It matches your eyes."

Ralph chuckled. "You think?"

"Connor has excellent taste."

"Come to think of it, you and I match," he said with a smile.

Just as he spoke, Connor walked into the bedroom wearing a tan suit. "Come on, you two. Everyone has started congregating out on the patio."

Jarod hoped that meant Sadie had arrived. He needed to tamp down the frantic pounding of his heart. He and his brother both linked arms with their grandfather and walked with him to the back of the house. Before they could see people, Jarod heard voices and smelled steaks cooking on the grill.

As they stepped out onto the patio, everyone clapped and sang "Happy Birthday." Jarod estimated the whole Bannock clan had showed up with at least twenty other family friends. His grandfather looked pleased with the turnout—sixty-odd people including grandchildren, young and old, sitting at the tables set up for the occasion.

Ralph thanked everyone for coming. "Go ahead and eat because that's what I intend to do. I'll bore you with a speech later!" His remarks drew laughter as Jarod and Connor helped him to his place at the head table.

"I'll get his food," Jarod said to his brother, who nodded.

He walked around the other side of the smorgasbord to fix his grandfather a plate. A quick glance at the assembled group revealed

the Hensons had come, but to his disappoint-
ment no Corkins or Lawsons yet. His gaze
traveled to Tyson and his wife's table, which
included Grant and Pat. No sign of Ned, either.

Jarod needed to keep the line moving. His
grandfather liked his steak medium-rare.
After filling the plate, he carried it to the
table and sat with him. Jarod wasn't hungry
and told Connor to go ahead and get his food.
His eyes went to Avery, looking particularly
lovely in a deep red dress. She moved around,
setting up a mike that could be passed around
for people to make toasts.

In another five minutes Ned showed up.
His father motioned him over to his table and
the two men got into a lengthy discussion.
Clearly, Grant wasn't happy about something,
but that was nothing new.

As Jarod continued to look around, he saw
Sadie and Zane slip in from the side of the
house to sit with Mac and Millie. Zane held
Ryan in his arms.

Sadie had dressed in a sophisticated orange, yellow and white print cocktail dress,
an outfit she'd probably worn to dinner in
San Francisco with some lucky man. The

short sleeves and scooped neck exposed the tan she'd picked up since moving back to the ranch. Her windblown blond hair had the luster of a pearl. Jarod could find no words.

Before long one of the caterers wheeled out a cart carrying a chocolate birthday cake with lighted sparklers. The cake was in the shape of a giant cowboy boot with the word *Ralph* written in red frosting down the side. More of Avery's doing. Jarod gave his sister a silent nod of approval.

Their grandfather did the honors of cutting the cake. To facilitate matters, Connor and Jarod helped pass the dessert. When he neared Sadie's table and she looked up, it struck Jarod how the years had added a womanly beauty to her that he found irresistible. He couldn't take his eyes off her. "Enjoy your meal?"

"It was delicious," she said in a quiet voice, but a glance at her nearly full plate told him she hadn't been hungry, either. "I brought a present for Ralph. Where shall I put it?"

"I'll take it for you and give it to him."

"Thank you." She handed him a gift bag. The touch of her fingers sent a live current through his body. He walked to the head table and put the small bag in front of his grandfather. "It's a gift from Sadie," he whispered, then went back to handing out the cake.

A little while later Avery announced it was time for people to give toasts. Using the mike, everyone got in on the act, telling anecdotes about Jarod's grandfather that brought smiles and laughter. Finally it was Ralph's turn. With their help, he got to his feet.

"What a gratifying sight! If only Addie could be here with me. Thank you all for coming to help me celebrate. I don't know what I'd do without my three wonderful grandchildren who made this night possible. It's a very special night because one of our long-lost neighbors, Sadie Corkin, has come back to us after an eight-year absence, along with her new little brother, Ryan, and his uncle, Zane Lawson. I look forward to us being neighbors for years to come."

Only Jarod understood the meaning behind his grandfather's words and loved him for it. After Ralph showed Jarod the card she'd given him, emotion swamped him to realize what a burden her father's hatred had been to her.

"Thanks for this, Sadie." Ralph held up the card shuffler. "Sadie used to play canasta with me and Addie. I look forward to another game soon. I taught her how to play, you know." He winked. "Maybe this time I'll slaughter *you* instead of the other way around."

Amid the laughter and cheering, Jarod saw Sadie smile. A few minutes later she got up from the table with Ryan, who'd become restless. Anticipating her departure, he asked Connor to take care of their grandfather, then excused himself to walk through the house and catch up to her out front. No way was she going to get away from him tonight. He'd been living for it. Zane was right behind her.

"Leaving so soon?"

She looked shocked at Jarod's approach. "I'm sorry to just slip out like that, but it's past Ryan's bedtime and he was getting too noisy."

"Understood." He darted the little boy's uncle a glance. "There's no need for you to leave, too, Zane. Stay as long as you want. There's going to be dancing. I know three unattached females at the party who've been dying to get to know you. Since my duties are done for the evening, I'll drive Sadie and Ryan home in my truck."

Zane's brows lifted. "Would that be all right with you, Sadie?"

"What do *you* think? You've done so much baby-tending, it's time you had a night off. Jarod's right about the ladies. What's nice is, they're *all* beautiful."

With a chuckle, Zane kissed Ryan, and after a thank-you to Jarod, he headed around the ranch house to join the party.

Sadie was trembling so hard, she was thankful she had Ryan to cuddle. For some reason Jarod had been alone tonight. She didn't know what that meant, but at the moment she didn't care because he wanted to take her home.

After she was settled, he reached around to fasten the two of them in with the seat belt. His nearness made her feverish. "I don't have a car seat for him, but I think we can manage to get you home without a problem."

"I'm not worried."

"Good." He shut her door and went around to the other side to climb in. "Your gift made Grandfather's night. Especially the card. He laughed till he cried."

"Cried would be the right word. My father pretty well ruined everyone's lives for years."

"Well, you're back where you belong and he couldn't be happier about it."

And you, Jarod? Are you happy about it, too?

Sadie wished she knew what was going on inside him. It wasn't long before they reached the ranch and she hurried inside with Ryan. Jarod followed. He'd never been allowed on Corkin property before, let alone to step across her threshhold. The moment was surreal for her.

"I'm trying to wean him off the bottle, but tonight he needs a little extra comfort after being around so many strange faces."

Jarod plucked him out of her arms. "Come on, Little Wants His Bottle." Sadie broke into laughter. "I'll change him while you get it."

There was no one in the world like Jarod. "I'm afraid he might not let you."

"We'll work it out, won't we," he said to Ryan. "I've changed my fair share of diapers at my uncle's house."

Delighted and intrigued to see him in this role, she left them alone long enough to half fill a bottle with milk. When she returned, she found Ryan ready for bed in a sleeper. There'd been no hystrionics. Jarod was holding him in his strong arms as they examined the animal mobile attached to the end of the crib. She paused in the doorway to listen.

"Dog," he told Ryan as he pointed.

"Dog," Ryan repeated. His blue eyes kept staring in fascination at Jarod.

"Now can you say horse?"

"Horse."

"That's right. One day you'll have a horse of your own."

Her eyes smarted. Jarod had always had a way with animals, but it was evident that the invisible power he possessed extended to little humans, too.

"I hate to break this up, but it's time to go night-night, sweetheart."

After she handed Ryan his bottle, Jarod lowered him into the crib. She tucked his rabbit next to him and Ryan started sucking on the nipple as he stared up at the two of them. Sadie went through her routine of singing his favorite songs to him. Pretty soon he'd finished most of the bottle and his eyes had fluttered closed.

They tiptoed out into the hall and went down to the living room. She turned to Jarod. "Thank you for helping me with Ryan. You were such a big distraction, he forgot to be upset."

A faint smile lingered at the corner of his compelling mouth. "I'm glad to know I'm useful for something."

She got this suffocating feeling in her chest. "I happen to know your grandfather couldn't get along without you."

They stood in the middle of the room. Jarod's eyes swept over her face and down her body, turning her limbs to water. "Do you realize this is the first time I've ever been inside your house, except at the funeral?"

"I was thinking the same thing, but I try not to let the ugliness of the past intrude. Ryan makes that a little easier."

"He's a sweet boy."

She could feel herself tearing up. "I just hope I'll be the mother he needs. It's a huge responsibility."

"You're a natural with him, Sadie."

"Thanks, but it's early days yet." Clearing her throat she said, "Shouldn't you get back to the party before Ralph is missing you?"

"Connor's with him. I don't need to be anywhere else tonight. What I'd like to do is continue a certain conversation that came to an abrupt end when we discovered Ned waiting for us after the rainstorm. Mind if I stay awhile?"

Jarod...

Sadie was terrified she was going to hear news that would ruin the rest of her life.

"Of course not. Please, sit down."

After all the years her father had spouted his hatred for Jarod, it was nothing if not shocking to see him take a seat on the couch and make himself at home, arms spread across the top of the cushions. She sat rigidly on one of the chairs in front of the coffee table opposite him.

"When you asked me how important Leslie Weston was to me, I had my reasons for not answering you at the time."

Here it comes, Sadie. "I should never have asked you that question."

He leaned forward. "You were right to ask. Leslie wouldn't have understood about Velvet. How is your filly, by the way?"

"Wonderful." She stirred restlessly on the chair. "Jarod...you don't owe me any explanations."

"Then you're not interested to know why Leslie wasn't at tonight's party with me?"

Sadie lowered her head. "It's none of my business."

"Don't play games with me, Sadie. There's too much history between us to behave like we're strangers."

"I agree," she confessed before eyeing him directly. "I thought she would be with you tonight. In fact, I was half expecting Ralph's birthday party would turn into an announcement of your engagement."

"You and a few other people, but it's never going to happen."

The finality of his words shocked her. "Why not?"

"We've stopped seeing each other."

Her heart ran away with her. "But I thought— I mean, I was led to believe your relationship was serious."

"I cared for her a great deal, but she wanted more from me than I could give her."

"You mean marriage."

"Yes. As long as we're being truthful, why don't you tell me how many men have proposed to you since you left Montana?"

There was no point in pretending there hadn't been men in her life after Jarod. "If any of them wanted to get married, I didn't give them a chance to get that close to me."

"Why not?"

She sucked in her breath. "Like you, I could tell they wanted a permanent relationship, but I wasn't ready to make a commitment."

For years she'd been in too much pain to even look at another man. When she finally did break down and start dating, no man came close to affecting her the way Jarod had done. He was an original. "How's that for honesty?"

"It's a start."

"Since we're going to be neighbors, I hope we can still be friends."

His black brows met in that fierce way they sometimes did. "That would be impossible."

His response was like a physical blow. "Why?"

"Because we've been lovers. There's no going back."

Heat suffused her cheeks. She shot to her feet. "That was a long time ago." She didn't want to talk about it.

"Too long. That's why we have to move forward. Marry me and it will be as if we were never apart."

"Jarod—" Maybe she'd just imagined he'd

articulated her greatest wish. Sadie thought she might expire on the spot.

"A very wise person said it best when describing you and me. Love means sharing a single soul."

Tremors ran through her. "Sounds like your uncle talking."

"You're wrong. It was Leslie. After being with you the other day, I went to see her and broke it off. In her pain she admitted it was pointless to love someone who couldn't reciprocate that love. I wanted to make it work with her, but it never happened."

Sadie shook her head, so incredulous she couldn't take everything in. "You don't know what you're saying. Too much time has gone by. You can't still be in love with me." She'd hurt him too deeply. He wasn't the same with her. "We're different people now. I have a little boy to raise."

Jarod was on his feet. "Maybe we've both been in love with a memory, nothing more. But the strength of that memory has prevented us from getting past it. You're a liar if you deny you didn't want to make love the other day while we were out riding."

She'd wanted it so badly, he would never know what she'd gone through to control herself.

He moved to the front door and turned to her. "I'm asking you to marry me, Sadie. In church. In front of everyone. We need to do it soon while my grandfather is still alive and able to give you away. Once we're married, we'll have time to fall in love all over again. If we don't, then we'll just deal with it." He was silent a moment.

"Think about it," he said at last. "Ryan needs a father. I need a wife. I want children. When you're ready to give me your answer, you know where to find me. But keep one thing in mind. I won't ask a third time. This is it."

Jarod was out the door like an escaping gust of wind without giving her a chance to answer him. *Without touching her.*

She stood there long after she'd heard the sound of his truck fade. He'd asked her to marry him for a second time, but he'd meant what he said. If she wanted him, she would have to go after him.

What was it Millie had warned her about a few weeks ago? *Don't you know about the great wounded warrior inside him? He needed you to believe in him.*

Sadie *did* believe in him. She was wildly in love with him. But it was clear he still wasn't sure about her. Not really. Otherwise he wouldn't have left so fast. He wouldn't have mentioned being married in church rather than on the reservation with his uncle Charlo doing the honors. He wasn't behaving like the Jarod she'd fallen in love with years ago.

It was up to her to prove her love for him. In the past they'd come together as equals. There'd been no need to chase because they'd been one. But that was back then. There was only one thing to do because she wanted the Jarod of eight years ago back again. The man who had no doubts about her, the man who'd ignored her father's threats and had come to steal her away to the reservation....

By the time Zane came home an hour later, she was out on the front porch waiting for him. "I'm glad you're back. Did you have a good time?"

"Yes. As a matter of fact I did." She heard a wealth of meaning behind his words that she intended to explore later. Right now she was in a hurry to find Jarod.

Zane studied her for a moment. "I'm surprised you're still up. What are you doing out here?"

"Waiting for you to get home. I need to go out again. Do you mind? Ryan's asleep."

"Of course I don't mind. But it's getting late. I'll worry about you being out alone."

"I'm just going to drive next door."

"Oh. Well, in that case…"

Zane didn't ask the obvious question. That was one of the reasons she loved him so much. "I'll only be as far away as my cell." She grabbed her purse.

With a subtle smile he handed her the keys. Sadie rushed past him to the truck.

When she arrived at the Bannocks and pulled up to the rustic ranch house, there were still half a dozen vehicles parked in front. Her heart raced to see Jarod's among them.

Making a quick decision, she walked around the side of the house, hoping to catch him helping with the cleanup. Instead, she ran into Connor, who was folding the round tables used for the dinner.

His eyes lit up in pleasure. "Hey! What are you doing back here?"

"I'm looking for Jarod."

"He's helping grandfather get to bed. I'll go tell him you're out here, but you're welcome to come inside."

"Thank you. I'll stay here."

He stacked the last table against the wall, then disappeared inside the house. She walked over to the swing and sat to wait. But it had grown cooler, so she got back up to move around.

"You wanted to see me?" Jarod's deep voice resonated inside her.

She swung around on her high heels. "I didn't hear you come out. Forgive me for intruding. Connor told me you were helping your grandfather, so if this isn't a good time, I'll come again."

He eyed her through shuttered lids. "If it was important enough for you to see me tonight, then let's not put it off." His terse comment alarmed her. "The temperature has dropped. Why don't we go back to your truck where you can be warm?"

Her truck wasn't the place she envisioned talking to him, but since he hadn't invited her in the house, it would have to do. She walked ahead of him, but was so nervous she stumbled several times on the rocky pathway. He was there to cup her elbow till they reached the Silverado.

Sadie climbed into the driver's seat. She had to hike up the dress she was wearing, and knew Jarod caught a glimpse of leg before he shut the door. She hoped he didn't think she was being provocative.

After he got in the other side, she said, "Where can we drive so there's no possibility of Ned watching our every move?"

"Is this going to take a while?" He sounded put out, but *was* he? Or could he be covering some hidden emotion? She had to find out.

Emboldened by her desperation to connect with the old Jarod, she turned to him. "Yes."

Something flickered in the recesses of his eyes. "How soon do you have to get back?"

"Zane's home for the night to take care of Ryan."

"Then we'll leave your truck here and take off in mine."

Sadie said a silent prayer of thanksgiving he was willing to listen to her. The next thing she knew he'd helped her down and walked her over to his truck. After opening the door, he gripped her waist without effort and lifted her into the passenger seat.

He drove them two miles up a badly rutted road that zigzagged behind the ranch house. It led to a shelter of pines where they could look down on the whole layout of the Hitting Rocks Ranch. Sadie had never been here before.

Jarod shut off the engine and shifted around, extending an arm along the back of the seats. She felt him tease her hair. "Old habits die hard. I have to reach farther to grab hold. Why did you cut your glorious hair?"

Sadie wasn't prepared for such a personal comment. "Off with the old seemed like a good idea after I got to California." She knew better than to ask him why he'd let his grow long. By doing so he'd made a statement that he was proud of his Crow heritage. It told Sadie's father and Ned Bannock to go to hell. She understood his feelings and loved him all the more for them, but she had to tread carefully right now.

He cocked his dark head. "All right. We're alone at last with no chance of being disturbed. Let's get this over with."

She'd been right. He didn't believe she believed in him anymore. "Why did you leave the house so fast? You didn't give me a chance to respond."

His searching gaze appraised her. "After the failure of our first attempt to become man and wife, I wanted to give you some breathing room before you made a decision about trying a second time. But it seems you didn't need it. Otherwise you wouldn't have come right over to the house again. I only need a one-word answer. Since I know what it is, I'll drive us back and send you home before it gets any later."

She moaned inwardly. "You're so sure of my answer?"

He grimaced. "The Sadie I once knew wouldn't have let me walk out of her house tonight."

Sadie took a deep breath. "The Jarod I once knew wouldn't have had to ask me to marry him a second time. He would have drawn me into his arms and told me we were going to get married as soon as it could be arranged."

His jaw hardened. "You spoke the truth earlier. Too much time has passed. We're different people now and can't go back."

"Isn't it sad that although our marriage didn't take place through no fault of our own, the fallout caused us to doubt each other. How does something like that happen?"

"We were young." His voice grated.

"That's not all of it, Jarod. Tell me something. What prompted you to ask me to marry you in a church in front of everyone?"

After a prolonged silence he said, "It's what every woman wants."

"That isn't what you planned for us the first time."

His body tensed. "I railroaded you into doing what I wanted. I thought I owned you. I believed you were mine. But I've since learned a man can no more own a person than he can the earth or the sky or the ocean."

Jarod's honesty touched her to the marrow. "How do you know it wasn't what I wanted, too? I would have given anything to have known your mother. You planned that wedding for us in her honor. It thrilled me. I've felt cheated ever since." Her heart was thudding out of control.

"You were too sweet and trusting, Sadie. I took advantage of you."

"Oh. So when you say we were too young, you really meant that *I* was too young to know my own mind."

"You weren't too young, but I know I influenced you."

"Don't you know you saved my life the day you found me sobbing on my horse? You helped me to know where to go with my sorrow. You comforted me. Every person could use that kind of influence. I was the lucky one to be able to turn to you.

"What saddens me is to realize that my being a Corkin caused you so much grief. To this day I wonder what I ever did for you to want me for your wife."

She had to wait a long time for the answer.

"Chief Plenty Coups taught that woman is your equal. She's a builder, a warrior, a farmer, a healer of the soul. All those qualities I found in you. That's what you were to me. I believed you loved me."

Jarod, Jarod. "Why past tense? I still do," she said. "That's never changed. It couldn't."

He'd turned his head to stare out the window. Sadie opened her purse and pulled out the bracelet he'd given her the night they'd made love.

"Jarod Bannock? Tonight you asked me to marry you. My answer is *yes,* but there's a condition. I want us to have the same ceremony you planned for us eight years ago."

Sadie got on her knees and moved across

the seat to lean toward him, getting in his face so he had to look at her. She dangled the beaded bracelet in front of him. "I want Uncle Charlo to marry us on the reservation. I want your family to be there along with the Hensons. In my heart I know your mother and father will be watching and they'll approve because they know how much I've always loved you."

She'd finally caught his attention.

"Before you fasten it around my wrist for a second time to make this official, there's something vital you need to know."

"You're talking about Ryan," he said, reading her mind.

"Yes. He comes with me."

His chest rose and fell. "You're both flesh of your mother's flesh. Do you think I could possibly love him any less?"

"No," she whispered, brushing his mouth with her own. "You have an infinite capacity for loving. I adore you, Jarod."

Chapter 8

Her words trickled through his mind and body like the wild, sweet Montana honey dripping from a honeycomb he'd discovered in a tree at the edge of the meadow years ago.

He studied the oval of her face, the passionate curve of her mouth so close to him he felt her breath on his lips. Moonlight illuminated the inside of the cab. Those solemn blue eyes were once again searching his. That was the way she used to look at him, as if he held all the answers to the universe.

"Aren't you going to put it on me?" He heard the slightest tinge of anxiety in her voice.

The bracelet.

She'd so mesmerized him, Jarod was slow to even breathe. He'd been convinced that when she'd fled to California, that token of his commitment had been lost or destroyed.

His fingers trembled as he caught the ends of the bracelet and fastened it around her wrist. The satisfying click echoed in his heart.

"Sadie—" Wrapping his arms around her, he lowered his mouth to hers the way he'd done eight years ago; a kiss he'd relived in a thousand dreams. Yet this was no dream. His loving, precious Sadie was back in his arms, alive and welcoming.

For a while those desolate years they'd been apart seemed to fall away while their minds and bodies communicated their need for each other.

"Darling," she murmured over and over again, as if she, too, was overwhelmed by such emotion.

Sometime later he tasted salt on his lips. "Your eyes are wet," he whispered against her lids.

"So are yours. I can't believe we're together again. It's been such a long, long time." Her tear-filled voice reached his soul. They clung to each other, attempting to absorb the quiet sobs of happiness that shook them both. "I'm so thankful we've found each other again. Jarod— You don't know. You just don't know."

"But I do." Jarod kissed the contours of her moist cheeks, then her mouth, never satisfied. She looked and tasted beautiful almost beyond bearing. Their desire for each other had escalated to the point they couldn't do what they wanted in the confined space of the cab.

"I want you, Sadie. I love you. I'm going to drive us back to the ranch. You'll stay with me tonight."

She moaned her assent as he helped her to sit up. "This is going to be a fast trip, so hold on!" Within seconds he started the engine and put the truck in gear to head down the road.

Sadie flashed him one of her disarming smiles. "We don't need to be in a hurry. My father's no longer on the lookout. The situation has changed and we've got the rest of our lives to be together."

He grasped her hand and kissed it. "That's what I thought the night I was coming for you. Never again will I take another moment of loving you for granted."

"Neither will I." Her voice shook. "How soon do you think we can be married? I don't want to wait."

That sounded like the exciting Sadie he'd thought had disappeared forever. "I'll talk to Uncle Charlo in the morning." June third would make the perfect wedding day. By then the deed to the Corkin ranch would be in Zane's hands, but Jarod wouldn't settle on an actual date with his uncle until Zane owned it free and clear.

"The dreams I've dreamed, Sadie. My grandfather's health has to hold out long enough to see our first baby come into the world. I can hardly wait to feel movement inside you."

She nestled closer to him. "Millie told me that if you and I had communicated, we'd probably have one or two little Bannocks by now. It's all I've been able to think of for days now."

"When I saw you at the graveside service holding Ryan, I was imagining you with our child. It shocked me how strong my feelings ran. Watching you with Ryan, I knew you'd be the sweetest mother on earth. The sooner we give him a brother or sister, the better. Connor and Avery kept me from being an only child."

How he'd love it if he and Sadie were the ones to give his grandfather his first great-grandchild. Ralph would be overjoyed. Tyson already had three. Jarod's uncle Charlo would be overjoyed, too. He'd carried a heavy burden over the years watching after Raven's headstrong son.

She pressed against him to kiss his jaw. "What's putting that secretive smile on your face?"

He squeezed her hand harder. "In January my uncle told me it was time to go on my vision quest at the top of North Pryor Mountain. It had to be in an area with risks like falling and contact with animals. The more rugged and mysterious the better."

"The snow would have been too deep!"

"It nearly was, but he told me I'd be guided. He said I possessed the power to achieve my ultimate destiny by using the senses and powers already given to me. After four days of fasting, I came back down and told him my mind was still clouded."

"Four days?" she cried. "I could never have done that."

"To be honest, nothing was worse than the way I felt when you never got in touch with me." Sadie buried her face against his shoulder. "My uncle told me my quest wasn't in vain. With more time all would be made clear, but I had to develop patience because everything else in my life had come too easily."

She lifted her head. "Too easily? You lost your mother, then your father and stepmother!"

"But I was given an uncle, grandparents and siblings, a home, money, education, good health. Grades came without effort. I had everything I wanted. And when I decided I wanted Sadie Corkin, I went after her. By some miracle I was able to snatch her away from all the other guys who were hot for her."

"Jarod!"

"That's the word for it, and I was the worst. I came up with a secret plan to marry the one girl in the county who was off-limits to me. I would have succeeded, too. But fate stepped in and taught me life's most bitter lesson."

Jarod covered her hand with his own. "When Ben told me your father had died, all I could think about was you rather than your loss. Suddenly my uncle's comment about my quest not having been in vain came into my mind."

She kissed the side of his neck. "There wasn't a day in my life that I didn't yearn to come home and find out why you'd stopped loving me. We've had to endure so much needless pain."

"Not only us. Everyone who loved us was affected, Sadie."

"I know. I'm still having trouble believing we're back together."

They reached the ranch house in record time. He pulled around in front and parked. After shutting off the engine, he reached out to hold her in his arms.

"By morning you'll believe it. Tomorrow when I ask my uncle to help prepare for our wedding, I'll thank him for being a great and wise man who guided me through my trials on the way to finding my ultimate destiny. He'll give me one of those long sober looks, as if he can see into the future, but I know he'll be smiling inside."

"I know the one you mean. That's how he looked at me the night he praised you. He couldn't love you more if you were his own son."

"That's how I already feel about Ryan," he whispered into her hair. "But right now I want to concentrate on us. I desperately need to love you all night."

She looped her arms around his neck and clung to him. "I've been thinking about that and would rather we went back to my house. Yours is full of family and they don't know about us yet. It might be a shock when Connor and Avery see us walk out of your bedroom in the morning."

"A happy shock because I've been impossible to live with. They'll get down on their knees to you for coming back to me." He bit gently on her earlobe. "Zane could be a different story."

"You're wrong. We have no secrets. Follow me home. Our being together won't shock him since he knows how long I've been ready to walk through fire for you. His one reaction will be relief that we've been able to find each other again after our painful history."

"Then let's not waste another second." He got out of the cab and went around to help her down. Knowing she was all his to love had made him euphoric. Their mouths fused before he swung her around and carried her over to her truck. After putting her inside he shut the door. "I'll be right behind you."

A shadow crossed over her face. "Promise me." She couldn't prevent the tremor in her voice. "If anything happened to you now…" He knew she was thinking of Ned.

"I'll sit on your bumper."

Her expression brightened before she started the engine. He retraced the steps to his truck and they formed a caravan to the Corkin property. Connor knew Jarod was with Sadie. He'd phone if there was an emergency with their grandfather.

Jarod checked his watch. It was ten to one. For the first time in their lives they had nothing to worry about except to love and be loved. As he followed behind her, he anticipated their true wedding night. She'd always been fascinated with the bygone traditions of his mother's people. The vision of disappearing into their own tepee after the ceremony wouldn't leave him alone.

After Sadie had parked in front of her place, she jumped down from the truck and held out her hand to him. When he reached her, she ran toward the porch, pulling him as if she were in the race of her life. They both were.

But she had to get the house key from her purse. When he saw how she was trembling, he reached for it. "Let me." Within seconds he'd found it. After unlocking the door, he opened it and followed her into the living room.

"Sadie?" A light went on and they discovered Zane standing near the the window.

She came to a halt. "Zane. Is something wrong with Ryan?"

That was Jarod's first thought, as well.

"No, but I'm glad you're both here because we need to talk. Mr. Bree emailed me to let me know he has a client coming by tomorrow at 9:00 a.m. to look at the house and property." His gaze flicked to Jarod. "A little while after that your cousin Ned came by. When he found out Sadie wasn't home he left, but I was afraid he'd wait for her outside so I've been keeping watch. I didn't phone because I knew the two of you were together."

She frowned. "What did he want?"

His mouth thinned into a tight line. "*He's* the client planning to buy the ranch and do a walk-through with the Realtor in the morning."

"But he's a Bannock!"

"That part of your father's will won't hold up in court."

"So that *criminal* who came close to murdering Jarod is planning to buy this ranch out from under us?" Her outrage was as real as Jarod's. "Over my dead body! How dare he come by here this late to trample over our lives!"

"My thoughts exactly," Zane muttered. "He claimed he was hoping to talk to you at the party, but he saw you leave with Ryan so he thought he'd still find you up."

Sadie's proud chin lifted. Jarod knew that look. "What did you tell him?"

"That I was buying the ranch and had already put down earnest money. He gave me a superior smile and said that unless I was paying more than $700,000, I didn't have enough money to close the deal."

"Neither does he. I'm not sure he has a dime to his name."

Zane's brows lifted. "That may be true, but I thought I'd better tell you that tonight because June third is only four days away. I think we'd better start looking for another ranch around here within our price range."

The woman at Jarod's side had gone quiet.

Much as he didn't want either Sadie or Zane to know what was going on behind the scenes, he needed to say enough to take the shattered looks off their faces. He put an arm around Sadie, pulling her close.

"He was bluffing, Zane. I do the ranching accounts. Sadie's right. Ned doesn't have any savings, and his father can't fund him any more loans. He certainly can't depend on his grandfather. Tyson has helped all his grand-children to the point he doesn't have that kind of money, either. He's using scare tactics, but it won't work. Your bid is right in the ball park so don't give up."

"We won't!" Sadie declared. "I know it's Mr. Bree's job, but it infuriates me to think he has the right to come here with Ned, who would do anything to hurt me for loving Jarod."

After her revealing explosion, Zane eyed the two of them with interest. "Why do I get the feeling you've got something to tell me?"

Sadie extended her arm. "Jarod put this bracelet back on me tonight. It's the one from his mother's family he gave me eight years ago. We're going to get married right away."

A broad smile lit Zane's face. "That the

best news I ever heard." He gave her a loving hug, then shook Jarod's hand. "When's the wedding?"

Jarod stared down at her. "As soon as it can be arranged."

"Good. It needs to happen fast. I have to tell you this girl has been dying for you."

"Zane—" Her blush warmed Jarod's heart. "You're the first person to know."

"When we've picked the date, we'll tell everyone. We plan to keep it to family only. My uncle will be marrying us out on the reservation."

"That sounds like heaven," Zane said. "Little Ryan's going to have an amazing dad who'll open fascinating new worlds for him."

Jarod picked up a nuance in the other man's tone. In truth Zane had been the only father Ryan had known since he was born. Zane loved his nephew deeply, and was one of the most genuine, likable men Jarod had ever met. But their news had just changed his world again. "I hope one day to live up to the hero uncle Sadie raves about."

"That's nice to hear. Thanks, Jarod. Now that you're both home safely and have heard the bad news, I'll go to bed."

Sadie gave him another hug before he left the living room. When she turned to Jarod he planted his hands on her shoulders. "I'm going to leave."

"No—" She flung herself at him. It reminded him of the night before they were to be married. She'd clung to him then, too, not wanting to be parted from him. "We're not going to let Ned ruin this night for us."

"He doesn't have the power."

"Then is it because of Zane being here?"

"No, Sadie." He kissed away her tears. "But it *does* have to do with him."

She shook her blond head in confusion. "What's changed since we came in the house?"

"He just found out we're getting married right away. In his mind the plans you two had to ranch together have suddenly gone up in smoke. He sees his nephew slipping away from him and fears he might not be able to buy the ranch, after all. You told me he moved here with you to start a new life after his divorce, but tonight we dropped a bomb on him."

"I know," she whispered. "I had no idea he'd still be up and waiting for me to come home. When we told him our news, there was a look in his eyes that haunted me."

"I saw it, too. You need to go to him before he's in bed and reassure him that whatever plans we make, he's included in them in every way. He's going to be a part of our family now, the same way my uncle Charlo and his family are a part of us. But a talk like that could take the rest of the night. Before you know it, Ryan will be awake."

"You're right, but I can't stand to see you walk out the door."

"The last thing I want to do is leave, but you two need your privacy to talk. Before I go, give me your phone so we can program each other's cell numbers."

Once that was accomplished he pulled her into his arms again. "Call me after Ned and the Realtor leave. Knowing Zane is with you, I'm not worried. I'll pick you and Ryan up. We'll drive over to tell grandfather our news."

Sadie clasped her hands on his face. "You're the most wonderful, remarkable man I've ever known. I didn't think I could love you any more before we came in the house. Now I can't find the right words to tell you what you mean to me. This will have to do until tomorrow." She pressed her mouth to his.

Though he wanted to devour her, he

couldn't do that while Zane was in the other room. The man was in a state of hell Jarod wouldn't wish on the retired SEAL. He'd already lived through a war both at home and in Afghanistan, and Sadie was the one person who could make things right for him.

She had no idea she held the hearts of three men in her hands. As she'd told him earlier tonight, Ryan came with her.

"See you in the morning." He kissed her once more, knowing she was in safe hands with Zane until Jarod could take care of her himself.

On the drive home, he decided that tomorrow morning he'd leave early for Billings to do some business at the bank and talk to Harlow Brigg. Jarod wanted the attorney to make his offer to Mr. Bree before the end of the day and get the transaction finalized. Zane and Sadie deserved good news and they were going to get it.

When he got back to the ranch, he set his alarm for six. He wouldn't get the sleep he needed, but it didn't matter. Until this business was over, he didn't have a prayer of relaxing.

The next morning after he'd showered and dressed, he knocked on Connor's door. Their bedrooms were upstairs across the hall from each other. Avery's was at the other end.

"Come on in." To Jarod's relief his brother was up and seated on the side of the bed, putting on his cowboy boots. Connor looked up at him with concern. "Is grandfather all right?"

"As far as I know. This is about something else. I need to talk to my best friend. That's you."

Connor looked taken aback. "You're mine, too."

"I realize I haven't shared some of my personal thoughts with anyone over the years, not even you. It's the way I'm made. But like grandfather and Avery, I've always known you were there for me. You've never pried or overstepped. I could always count on you."

"Ditto. I wouldn't have made it through my divorce without you."

Jarod nodded. "We've been lucky to have each other. That's why I want to confide in you now."

Connor sat forward. "You sound so serious. What's bothering you, bro? After last night I figure this must have to do with Sadie." Connor eyed him with compassion. "Are the rumors true about her and Zane Lawson?"

Jarod caught a leg of the chair with his boot, pulled it forward and sat. "No. Last night I asked her to marry me for the second time and she said yes."

Connor jumped off the bed in shock. "Second time—"

"The first time was eight years ago. We'd planned for Uncle Charlo to marry us on the reservation. The ceremony was all arranged in secret so Daniel wouldn't get wind of it. Grandfather and I wanted to protect you and Avery. I was on my way to pick Sadie up with the horse trailer the night the accident happened."

For the next twenty minutes he filled his brother in on everything, including the tragic misunderstanding that had sent Sadie to her mom's in California.

"All these years Sadie thought her father was behind it, but that wasn't the case."

His brother shook his head in disbelief.

"The person who rammed me in the side of my truck had every intention of putting me out of commission. I didn't know until recently it was a deliberate act and I have what I call partial proof."

"*What?*"

Jarod reached into his pocket and then handed Connor the sheet of paper from the body shop in Bozeman. "Notice the date. The accident happened the night Sadie turned eighteen."

"Owen Pearson? But he's—"

"Ned's friend?" Jarod supplied.

Connor's expression turned dark. He walked around the room for a minute, rubbing the back of his neck. Then he turned to Jarod.

"I always thought there was something wrong about that day. When the hospital called, the whole family went en masse to visit you. Avery and I were terrified you might die. Both grandfather and your uncle Charlo must have aged ten years. But the only one who didn't show up was Ned.

"I remember Uncle Grant being particularly upset because Ned wasn't anywhere around. He tried to call him all day but Ned didn't answer his mobile phone. None of the hands knew his whereabouts and none of his friends had seen him, not even Owen. He didn't show up at the ranch until late the next night."

By now Jarod was on his feet. "Did the police question him?"

"I don't know, but I heard Uncle Grant say later that he'd had a date with one of the girls who worked at her mom's beauty salon in White Lodge. Rose, or Rosie? I can't remember. That's why he hadn't heard about the accident."

Jarod frowned. "I saw his Jeep in town that evening. It might be worth checking her out to see if she knows anything about that night."

"Do it, Jarod. Too many times I've wanted to strangle Ned with my bare hands for his treatment of you. If we could prove he or Owen was at the wheel of Owen's truck that night…"

"I plan to find out," Jarod's voice was harsh. "Did you know he's trying to buy the Corkin ranch?"

"Say that again?"

"Daniel didn't will it to Sadie. He put it up for sale. Ned's already found out about it."

"Our cousin?" Connor exploded with an angry laugh. "That's not only impossible, it's absurd!"

"He's going over there this morning with Bree from Parker Realty to make the inspection before he puts down the money."

"*What* money?"

"Tyson told Grandfather he's going to take

out $700,000 for him. Uncle Grant believes if he has his own place, he'll become responsible and turn into a rancher."

Connor put up his hands. "Wait a minute here. You mean, Grandfather's okay with that?"

"No. He has his own plan working." Once again Connor was a captive audience while Jarod explained about Harlow's part in the private purchase. "We're making sure Zane ends up owning it. I'm going into Billings right now to see him."

Lines marred Connor's features. "Happy as I am to hear that, Ned's not going to take this lying down, especially when he finds out you and Sadie are getting married."

"That's why I've got to nail him for the accident. Once I know the whole truth, I'll confront him and put the fear in him about having to do some serious jail time. Thanks to your recall about the night I was in the hospital, I've got a valuable piece of information that could be the proof I need to implicate him." He hugged his brother. "I owe you."

Three hours later he'd finished his business and finalized the details of the purchase with Harlow Brigg.

On his way back to the ranch, he phoned his uncle and broke the news. Charlo sounded elated, which didn't happen very often. They talked about possible dates for a ceremony and would make a final decision in the next few days.

When Jarod passed through White Lodge, he stopped at the Clip and Curl beauty salon. The sign said they welcomed walk-in traffic. He got out of his truck and entered the shop. The women stared at him as he approached the counter.

His gaze darted to the license on the wall. It belonged to a Sally Paxton. Her name meant nothing to him, but Jarod was determined to get answers. If this lead didn't reveal any new information, he planned to go to the Pearson ranch to confront Owen.

An older beautician washing a client's hair looked up. "Hi! I've never seen you in here before."

"I usually get my hair cut on the reservation. Does someone named Rose work here?"

"If you mean Rosie, that's my daughter over there."

A dark blond woman who looked to be Avery's age was sweeping the floor after the last client. She looked up at him. "You want to see me?"

"I was told you do a great job so I thought I'd come in."

"Who said that?"

"I heard someone telling the new vet over at Rafferty's."

"You mean Liz Henson?" He nodded. "That's nice to hear. We were part of a group of girls who hung out in high school, but she was usually barrel racing."

"I learned she's going to compete at the world championship in Las Vegas."

"Isn't that great? Be with you in a second. Go ahead and sit in the chair."

Jarod did her bidding. "I'm getting married soon and need the ends of my hair trimmed. Just an inch." This would be a new experience for him. Before he'd let his hair grow, he used to ask Pauline, Uncle Charlo's wife, to cut it.

She smiled. "Lucky woman." After fastening the cape around his neck, she undid the thong. "Do you know how many females would kill for gleaming black hair like this?"

"I hope not."

With a chuckle, Rosie washed and combed it before getting out the scissors. He noticed she wore a wedding ring. "You know I always admired Liz."

Glad he didn't have to get her back on the subject, he said, "Why do you say that?"

"She was serious about school and didn't drink like some of the girls."

"You're talking about the famous keg parties. Even though I graduated before your time, I heard they got pretty wild with Owen Pearson and Ned Bannock around."

"Ned was the ultimate party animal."

"Were you two an item?"

"That's a laugh. Do you remember a girl named Sadie Corkin? She barrel raced with Liz. All the guys were nuts about her."

His breath caught. "I remember hearing about her."

"Ned had it bad for her, but she couldn't stand him and every girl knew it. She moved right before graduation. It was weird her going away like that before she got her diploma."

You'll never know, Rosie.

After she'd tied his hair back again, he winked at her. "So you never dated him?"

"Are you kidding? Guys like that are toxic."

So that was another of Ned's lies. Jarod

wondered why the police hadn't interrogated Rosie, but he was going to find out.

"You were wise to stay away."

She undid the cape. "My boyfriend made sure of it."

"Good for you." He pulled forty dollars out of his wallet and put it on her table. "You did a great job. When I need another haircut, I'll be back."

"Congratulations on your upcoming wedding."

"Thank you, Rosie."

Chapter 9

Sadie stood by to watch while Ned and Mr. Bree walked through the house inspecting everything. She could only imagine how much Jarod's cousin was enjoying this. The Corkin property had always been off-limits to the Bannocks. Now it was up for sale and Ned was sure he was going to become the new owner of Farfields.

But Jarod had assured her it wouldn't happen. Sadie believed him, which was the only reason she could stomach this vile intrusion into her life. She continued to watch in disgust as he handled her father's firearms. Before the funeral Mac had moved them from Daniel's bedroom to the hall closet, where they'd been locked up for safe keeping. Millie had insisted that with a child in the house, they would keep all the ammunition stored at their place.

"This is a fine collection." He flashed Sadie a strange smile. "Your father really knew his guns. I plan to buy a permanent display case for them."

There's something wrong in his head. That's what Jarod had told her years ago. Ned Bannock *was* mentally ill. A shudder racked her body.

"I believe we're finished here." Mr. Bree spoke up. Sadie immediately locked the closet. "Thank you for allowing us into your home, Ms. Corkin. We'll see ourselves out."

She nodded and followed them. Through the window she watched them drive away in a car with the Parker Realty logo on the side. Without wasting a second she rang Zane, who was on his way back from White Lodge with the Hensons and Ryan.

The Hensons were overjoyed to hear the news about Sadie and Jarod, but they still didn't know about her father's will and Sadie intended things to stay that way. Zane had taken Mac and Millie to breakfast with him and Ryan, not only to get them all away from the ranch while Ned was here, but to offer the Hensons a business proposition since he would be helping Sadie run the ranch.

Jarod had been so right about Zane. Last night she and Zane had talked for several hours until Sadie had convinced him nothing was going to change, only get better.

In a few minutes he came through the back door holding Ryan. Millie followed them inside. When Zane lowered him to the floor, Ryan grabbed him around the leg, wanting to be picked up again. "Hey, sport." Zane lifted him in the air with a happy laugh Sadie hadn't expected to hear again after he'd left her and Jarod last night.

Millie darted Sadie a secret smile. Nothing got past her.

As he poured some juice for Ryan, Millie pulled Sadie into the front room. "When Zane told us the news, Mac and I were so happy, we almost burst!"

"You need to hear the whole story." After Sadie quickly filled her in she said, "I have to tell you, this bracelet worked its magic. Bless you for holding on to it all this time."

She hugged Millie hard. "Without it, I don't know how long it would have taken me to break through that stoic barrier he sometimes erects."

"Maybe another ten minutes?" Millie quipped. "I can't wait to tell Liz. She left early to help with a foaling problem on the Drayson ranch."

"I'll phone her after I call Jarod."

"It's going to make her realize that if this can happen to her sister, it will happen to her, too, when the time is right."

"Of course it will. Oh, Millie. I can't believe this day has come. I never dreamed it would."

"Does Ralph know?"

She shook her head. "We're planning to tell him our news as soon as Jarod picks me up."

"Then don't waste another second. If you or Zane need me, just give me a call."

"You've already helped us so much."

"I wish you'd been there for breakfast when Zane asked Mac to teach him how to be a rancher. My husband could hardly talk he was so flattered."

"Zane's going to learn from the best."

"Honey—" She put a hand on her arm. "I'm sorry about your father, but I have to say how happy I am your mom ended up with Tim Lawson. I really like his brother."

"Me, too. Men like him and Jarod don't come along more than once in a century."

"You can say that again."

"And of course, I include Mac in that group."

Millie laughed, but Sadie could tell she was pleased.

While Ryan was still in the kitchen with Zane, Sadie walked in her bedroom to phone Jarod. He picked up on the first ring. "You must be psychic," he said. "I was just going to phone you. I'm one minute away from your door."

"I can't wait! I'll grab Ryan and meet you outside."

After renewing her lipstick and running a brush through her hair, she put on her cowboy hat. Once she'd stowed some diapers and small toys in her purse, she flew through the house to the kitchen. Millie must have gone home.

"Come on, cutie. I hate to tear you away from your uncle, but we're going with Jarod so you can get acquainted with your new grandfather-to-be."

Zane gave him a kiss. "See you later, sport."

Sadie rushed through the house and out the front door with Ryan. She was greeted with one of those ridiculous wolf whistles. Coming from Jarod, it was a total surprise. He was already out of the truck and had opened the rear door. 'You look good enough to eat."

"Jarod…" She moved closer, melting from the look he gave her. "Oh, you got him a car seat!"

"I picked it up in town on the way home." He took Ryan from her arms and strapped him in. "Hey, little guy. Remember me? We're going for a ride."

Ryan had fastened his attention on Jarod, but he didn't cry. Once they'd closed the door, Sadie and Jarod reached for each other. Jarod pressed her against the side of the truck, causing her hat to fall off. She didn't care. Their emotions were spilling all over the place. It wasn't until Ryan started to get worked up over being ignored that Jarod lifted his hungry mouth from Sadie's, eliciting a protest from her. She was finding it impossible to let him go.

He looked different somehow. "Did you do something to your hair?"

"You noticed. There's a story behind it. I'll tell you about it later." He picked up her hat and helped her into the cab. After talking to Ryan and handing him a toy, Sadie pressed against Jarod for the short drive to the ranch.

"Tell me what went on with Ned."

A shudder ran through Sadie. "When he was handling one of the rifles, I was so sickened by him, I couldn't watch. He acted as if he already owned the place."

"It'll never happen."

"I believe you."

"Thank God." He put his arm around her and stopped long enough to give her a deep kiss before they ended up in front of the ranch house. Once inside, the housekeeper made a fuss over Ryan, who clung to Sadie.

"I'm sorry, Jenny. He's still getting used to people."

"That's natural."

"How's Grandfather?"

"Feeling so spry he gave Martha the day off. He's out on the patio having lunch. I'll bring some for you, too."

"Thanks."

Jarod led Sadie down the hall and out the door to the covered patio where'd they celebrated his birthday. His grandfather's gray eyes brightened when he saw them. "Well, look at the three of you."

"Hi, Ralph. I can tell you're feeling much better." She kissed his cheek. "You saw Ryan before, but now he'd like to meet you."

"You're a good-looking little fella, aren't you?" He rubbed Ryan's head. "Just like your mom and sister. Sit down and join me."

Jarod helped her to get seated at the glass-topped table. She held Ryan on her lap while Jarod took his place next to her. Jenny brought out two more salads and rolls and glasses of iced tea.

"We're glad you're up because we have an announcement to make."

Ralph preempted him. "About time, too! When's the wedding?"

On cue, tears filled her eyes. "You know?"

"I knew the second I saw your faces just now. It's written all over you."

She reached out to squeeze his hand. "Does that mean you're happy about it?"

"Ah, honey, you know Addie and I were always crazy about you. So was my grandson. Otherwise he wouldn't have made preparations for your marriage the first time around."

Sadie lowered her head. "Jarod's accident changed our lives."

"Indeed it did, but that period is over."

They spent much of lunch talking about plans for the ceremony on the reservation. But after two hours Ryan got restless and it was time to take him home. Once Ralph was settled on the swing with his bifocals and the latest ranching magazine, Jarod picked up Ryan and they made their way back out to the truck.

He shot her an all-consuming glance. "I think it's time for everyone to have a good nap."

Her heart did somersaults as they pulled away from the ranch. But when his cell phone rang and he picked up to answer, her excitement was short-lived. A fierce expression crossed his face, the one that caused her legs to shake.

"What's wrong?" she asked as soon as he'd ended the call.

"It's nothing for you to worry about."

She sat straighter. "How would you like it if our positions were reversed and I said the same thing to you?"

He expelled a troubled sigh. "That was Ben. Fire has broken out in one of the sheds on the

property. I've got to go, but I'll be back." As
soon as they reached the Corkin ranch house,
Sadie jumped out to get Ryan with Jarod's
help. "We had a good time today, didn't we,
little guy?" He lowered the toddler to the
ground.

Sadie looked up at Jarod. "Please be careful."

"Always." He gave her a hard kiss before getting back in the truck. As he pulled
away, she realized the Silverado was gone.
Zane must have gone to town. This would
have been the perfect opportunity for her and
Jarod to enjoy alone time, but it would have
to come later.

Much as she hated to see him go, there
was something she needed to do. After she
gave Ryan a bath she put him down for his
nap, then got on the phone to speak to her
heart doctor in California. His nurse said he
wouldn't be able to return her call until after
five California time. Sadie would have to wait.

Jarod wanted children. So did she. That was
why this call was necessary because he didn't
know about her arrhythmia.

Sadie was feeding Ryan dinner in his high
chair when the phone rang at ten to six. She

glanced at the Caller ID and picked up. "Dr. Feldman?"

"Is this Sadie Corkin?"

"Yes. Thank you for returning my call so fast."

"How are you?"

"Wonderful. I haven't had any problems since you put me on this last medication."

"That's excellent."

"The reason I'm calling is that since mother's passing, I've moved back to Montana and now I'm getting married to the man I told you about."

"What a lucky man. That's splendid news!"

"You can't imagine how happy I am, but he wants a baby soon. So do I. What do you think about my getting pregnant? After what happened to mother, I have to admit I'm frightened."

"It goes without saying you have to keep taking your medication and use a reliable form of birth control until you've seen a specialist. Let me assure you there's a whole new type of procedure for your kind of problem that's had a high success rate."

For the next few minutes he went on to describe the benefits and risks. "Where are you in Montana?"

"Near Billings."

"I'll look on my index. Let me give you the name of a specialist there, Dr. George Harvey, who performs procedures for your particular heart condition. I advise you to get an appointment right away. I'll send your medical records."

"Thank you so much, Dr. Feldman."

"You're welcome. I want to hear back and know what's going on with you."

"Of course." She hung up.

A whole new type of procedure?

How would Jarod feel if she had it done before they were married? But what if she went through with it and it didn't work? Haunted by all the what-ifs, she cleaned Ryan's face and hands before taking him outside for a walk.

She hadn't heard from Jarod yet and was starting to get worried. A few minutes later Zane pulled up in front of the ranch house. He got out of the truck and picked up Ryan, who was thrilled to see him.

Sadie smiled at him. "Where have you been?"

"Bozeman."

"How come?"

"I've been looking up job opportunities on the internet and came across an ad put out by the Bureau of Land Management. I decided to go in for an interview."

Sadie had thought he wanted to learn to be a rancher. Her surprise must have shown.

"Hey, don't worry. I'm not planning to go anywhere. I can combine ranching with another job."

"You're going crazy around here already, aren't you?"

"No. I love it here, but I want to find something where I can use some of my skills, too."

"What kind of work was the BLM advertising for?"

"They need uniformed rangers to provide law enforcement support. Because of my military training, I'm a natural for it. At the moment there's an opening in northeastern Montana. Naturally I don't want to go there. But I've learned there may be an opening soon with the national Community Safety Initiative for American Indians in this area so I can stay home on the ranch. On my days off I'll work with Mac."

"What would you do exactly?"

"Work on eradicating drugs, investigate criminal trespassing and theft of government property including archaeological and paleontological resources. When I was talking to Jarod's sister last night, she told me there's a great need for that kind of protection around the archaeological sites. She also told me about one of the rangers up in Glasgow who apprehended a sniper after several people had been killed."

Yup. That sounded like it was right up Zane's alley. Sadie smiled inside. So that was what Zane meant when she'd asked him if he'd had a good time at the birthday party and he'd said yes. He'd been talking to Avery. Had she been the one to spark his interest in a BLM job?

In school Avery had been known as the Ice Queen. Like Jarod, she had a regal aura about her that in her case intimidated guys who'd wanted to ask her out. Not Zane. Sadie bet he'd danced with her as long as he'd felt like it.

"Sounds like an exciting prospect."

"Maybe. I've still got more research to do before I jump in." He flicked her a glance. "Is Jarod coming over?"

"Yes, but there's been a fire on Bannock

property and he had to go. I still haven't heard from him. He's got to be all right, Zane."

"Nothing's going to happen to him. Have you fed Ryan?" She nodded. "Good. Why don't I put him to bed and give you a break?"

"Are you sure?"

"Positive."

"Then I'll let you, because I haven't visited Velvet all day." She hugged both of them. "My horse needs a daily walk around the corral and some loving."

His eyes danced. "Don't we all. You're lucky."

She grinned all the way to the barn. It appeared that finding a job that appealed to Zane had changed his whole outlook. After a career as a navy SEAL she'd feared he would never find anything as challenging. But this evening he looked and sounded happier than she'd ever known him to be.

Sadie was so glad for him and so in love with Jarod she thought her heart would burst. It must be a bad fire, otherwise he would never stay away from her this long and torture her. She prayed he wasn't in danger. *Please come home soon, darling.*

Chapter 10

Jarod and Connor, along with Ben, their uncle Grant, two of their cousins plus other ranch workers, stood outside the smoldering heap that had been one of their hay storage sheds until a couple of hours ago. At one point Jarod had gotten out the backhoe to tear down part of the shed so the firefighters could finish extinguishing the flames.

The fire marshall walked over to them.

"It was a set fire."

"Damn," Grant muttered.

That wasn't a surprise to Jarod. There'd been no lightning, no faulty electrical wir-

ing. Just pure arson. Luckily the shed had only
been a third full and the fire hadn't spread to
the other buildings. A fifty-thousand-dollar
loss. Jarod couldn't help think of the sense-
less waste of man hours and valuable hay for
the cattle. A new shed would have to be built.

"Have you got any enemies?"

Jarod could think of one and shared a silent
message with Connor.

Their uncle shook his head, not saying a
word, but he had to be worried his youngest son hadn't come running when the fire
had broken out. Ned, who was supposed to
be working in a nearby building, should have
been one of the first to see the flames.

But his cousin wasn't anywhere around.

Jarod knew Ned wanted to buy Sadie's
ranch, but if he'd found out someone had
gotten in ahead of him with more money, he
would have had plenty of time to light a fire
in retaliation against his father and Tyson.

Connor and Jarod returned to the house,
and Connor seemed to have read his brother's mind.

"We need to confront Uncle Grant and
Tyson about the fact that Ned was nowhere

around. Grandfather will hate it, but this can't wait."

"Agreed," Jarod replied grimly. "Particularly since I visited the beauty shop this morning and learned from Rosie she never dated Ned. He couldn't have been with her the night of my accident. Your tip gave me the proof I needed that his alibi was a lie."

"Do you suppose Ned found out he was outbid?"

"I do. Since our bid came in at $720,000, Bree probably phoned him to give him the bad news as soon as possible and Ned lost it."

"He's probably at the bar in town getting drunk."

"Maybe." But Jarod had a dark feeling and felt a cold sweat break out. "Let's talk to Uncle Grant right now. We'll go in my truck."

They headed for Tyson's ranch house half a mile away. Grant and his family were on the porch talking as Jarod and Connor got out of the truck and walked toward them.

"Have any of you seen Ned?" Jarod asked the question of all of them, but he was looking at his uncle.

"Not since breakfast."

"We're pretty sure Ned lit that fire," Connor said. "We also know that today he was outbid for the Corkin ranch. Someone else is buying it."

"Who?"

"Zane Lawson—he wants to be around to help raise Sadie's little brother."

"That's as it should be," Tyson murmured. He sounded a lot like Ralph just then.

Jarod nodded. "Ned's rage has been building for a long time, Uncle Grant. I have proof he had something to do with my accident eight years ago."

"What do you mean?"

He pulled the receipt from his wallet and handed it to his uncle. His cousins looked at the paper along with their father. "Notice the date. Call Owen's father and ask him about that Ford truck. The police would be interested to see the vehicle that almost got me killed.

"Ned used to follow me when I rode into the mountains to meet secretly with Sadie. His jealousy crossed the line. I never told you about those times. That was my mistake."

His uncle weaved silently in place.

"Today I learned that the excuse he made up about being with Rosie from the beauty shop in town that night was a lie. She never dated him. For some reason the police didn't follow up his story with her. You do realize that every time something bad happens, Ned isn't around and can't account for his whereabouts. His drinking problem is another indication that something's off. He needs psychiatric help and has for a long time. You know it, and we know it."

Grant looked shattered.

"You never had control over him. That part I've always been able to handle. But burning down the hay shed has endangered everyone, not to mention the financial loss. Tyson and Ralph are old and failing in health. I don't want them to be hurt by this."

Grant looked at his sons in alarm. "Boys? We've got to find him."

"We'll all help." Connor had fire in his eyes.

"Let's go." Jarod raced for his truck. When Connor joined him he said, "Before we look anywhere, I need to make sure Sadie is all right." His wheels spun as he took off for her ranch.

"If he has gone after her, at least Zane is

there," Connor reasoned. "Ned would be no match for a former SEAL."

"You're right." Jarod broke the speed limit getting to Farfields. Relief swamped him when he saw the Silverado parked out front. "I'll be right back."

He jumped out of the truck and knocked on the front door. After a minute Zane answered. He smiled at Jarod. "You look and smell like you've been battling a forest fire, but Sadie will be so happy to see you, she won't care."

"I hope not. Is she inside?"

"No. She went down to the barn about an hour ago to exercise Velvet. You'll find her there or out in the corral. She's crazy about that horse."

"Thanks, Zane."

He ran back to the truck. "Connor? Come with me."

His brother got out. "Where are we going?"

"To the barn. Zane said she's there, but it's getting late. I've got a feeling something's wrong."

They made their way on foot and checked the corral. No sign of her. Putting a finger to his lips, Jarod walked around to the front of the barn. The doors were closed. On a warm evening like this she would have kept them open. Jarod felt the cold prickle of sweat on the back of his neck as the dark feeling returned.

Sadie was ready to leave after walking Velvet back to her stall when she saw Ned standing there, a dangerous glint in his eyes. She'd seen it before and shuddered. There was no reason why he would be here except for a bad one. Aware she was alone, she felt a dual sensation of fear and nausea rise up in her.

"I don't know what you're doing here, but you're not wanted," she said, trying not to show how frightened she was. "Get away from the doors, Ned. I have to get back to Ryan."

Jarod's cousin had a strong physique like his father. She could try to push him away, but she couldn't stand the thought of touching him. He'd been drinking. She could smell it.

"No, you don't. Zane's there. We've got this whole barn to ourselves." His looks were attractive enough, but the way he leered at her made her cringe.

"Jarod will be here any minute."

"No, he won't." He gave her that insidious smile. "He's putting out a fire."

The mention of it alarmed her. "How do you know about that?"

"I'm a Bannock, remember? Anything that goes on at the ranch I know about. What I'm here to find out is what you know about the buyer who outbid me for your father's ranch."

"What do you mean?"

"Bree called me this afternoon and told me he sold the ranch to someone else for $720,000. That kind of money doesn't grow on trees."

Her heart lurched. Zane's $700,000 bid had never stood a chance.

"I didn't learn the buyer's name, but the only person I know around here who can fork out that much cash is my half-breed cousin. He's a wealthy son of an injun, did you know that?"

"Don't you ever call Jarod that again." She almost spat out the words. "If he is wealthy, it's through hard work, something you don't know anything about."

Ned laughed. "O-oh. You're beautiful when you're angry, you know? But I'll do and say whatever the hell I feel like. Looks like he got what he wanted. There's oil under your land. He knows it, and he's been biding his time, waiting for you to fall into his hand like a ripe plum. Next thing we know he'll be drilling."

Sadie's body went rigid. There was no oil, but he wasn't listening. "What did he ever do to you?"

Ned cocked his head. "He got born."

"Jarod has as much right to life as you."

"Nature made a mistake."

Incredible. "Is that why you decided to drive Owen's truck into Jarod's eight years ago?"

His smirk faded. "What are you talking about?"

"You know exactly. I can see it on your face. You followed him from White Lodge and picked your spot to ram him."

"Yeah. I did a pretty good job if I say so myself. He had it coming. But even if he could prove it, there's nothing he can do about it. The statute of limitations on that hit-and-run case ran out a long time ago."

She shook her head. "You could have killed your own flesh and blood."

"Nah. Don't you know an injun has nine lives like a cat?"

Ned had lost touch with reality.

"The body shop in Bozeman has proof Kevin Pearson's truck was taken in to be repaired the morning after the accident. Jarod showed me a copy of the receipt. You paid cash. With that evidence, I'll go to the police and reopen the case myself!"

His cruel smile sickened her. "Well, then, honey, before you do that, I might as well take what you've been giving to that no good bum."

He lunged for her and dragged her into one of the empty stalls, knocking her down.

Sadie screamed at the top of her lungs, upsetting the horses, who whinnied. He covered her mouth with a hand that smelled faintly of gasoline and climbed on top of her.

"You fight like a she-cat. What does that long-haired cousin have that I don't? Come on, baby." He'd straddled her. "It's time you showed me what you've got. You need to share. I've waited long enough. This is going to be fun."

With her wrists pinned above her head in one hand, he ripped at the front of her blouse with the other, stifling her screams with his mouth.

Using every ounce of strength, she bit him as hard as was humanly possible. Warm salty blood filled her mouth.

"Ack! You little—" But she didn't hear another word because he was silenced by someone bigger and stronger who seemed to have come out of nowhere.

Ned spewed his venom, but it did no good. It was Jarod who had pulled him off her and now had him on the ground facedown in a hammerlock.

Connor was there, too. Together they tied his wrists and ankles with rope. The sheriff walked in on them as Jarod looked up at her. She'd never seen such fear in those black eyes. "Are you all right?"

"Yes." She tried to cover herself with the torn fabric of her shirt. "You got here just in time."

"Thank God." Jarod turned the sheriff. "We're glad you're here."

While Connor guarded Ned, the sheriff took her statement. Jarod led her outside before wrapping her in his arms. His body trembled like hers. "If anything had happened to you..." he murmured into her hair.

"He needs psychiatric help."

"That's what I told Uncle Grant earlier. We all knew who set fire to the hay shed. You're safe now and this whole ugly business is finally over. Come on. Let's get you home so you can shower and get cleaned up."

She buried her face against his chest as they made their way toward the house. "I was so terrified."

"So was I when I heard your scream, but he'd rigged something against the doors from the inside so we had to climb in through the rear window to get to you."

"Oh, Jarod." Sadie broke down sobbing. "How did you know where to find him?"

"A strong hunch. He'd lost everything else. Knowing how his mind works, I suspected he'd come after you. Rest assured he'll never bother you or anyone else again."

An anxious Zane came hurrying down from the porch. "What's happened?" He sounded frantic.

"She's all right, Zane. Ned decided to pay her a visit in the barn, but Connor and I got there in time and now he's tied up. The sheriff's with them."

"Sadie—" The other man gave her forehead a kiss. "I'll go see what I can do to help."

While Zane took off at a run, Jarod entered the house and walked her through to her bedroom. "You've got blood all over you."

"I bit him so hard, I don't know if he has a bottom lip left."

He hugged her to his heart. "You're my warrior woman all right."

She let out a shaky laugh. "He'll need stitches."

"He'll need a lot more than that. My brave Sadie. You had to deal with him all those years."

"You've had to endure much worse, almost losing your life. He admitted to running into you with Owen's truck, but I don't think Owen was with him. He's insane."

"Shh. That's all behind us now." He stopped in front of the bathroom door. She felt his eyes rove over her, searching for marks and bruises. "What can I get for you?"

"Not a thing. My robe is on the door. I'll be out in a minute. Don't go anywhere!"

"As if I would. I'll be in the living room."

She clung to him until he walked away. After a shower and shampoo, followed by a vigorous brushing of teeth, she emerged from the bathroom feeling rejuvenated. No more

Ned. That thought was enough to erase the horror of her experience.

Once she'd dressed in a clean pair of jeans and a cotton sweater, she entered the living room, where everyone had gathered, including the sheriff who needed to bag her clothes for the forensics lab. Jarod reached for her and put his arm around her shoulders.

Now that she was no longer terrified, she saw the soot on his arms and face. The shiny black hair she'd noticed earlier no longer gleamed due to the debris from the fire. Both he and Connor smelled of smoke.

The sheriff nodded to her. "Ms. Corkin? We're sorry to hear about the assault, but are thankful to learn you're all right. Mr. Bannock has been taken into custody and his family notified. If you don't mind my asking you some more questions, I'll leave as soon as we're through."

"That's fine." The next few minutes passed in a blur. After statements were taken, the sheriff left.

Sophie's gaze swept over the man she worshipped. "You and Connor fought a fire today and look absolutely exhausted. This is one time when I want you to go home. You need food and a shower in that order."

All three men chuckled.

Jarod's white smile shone through the grime left by the fire. "You mean you don't like me just the way I am?"

Her eyes smarted. "You know better than to ask me that question, but I'm thinking of your comfort. Please come right back. I'll be counting the seconds."

"Watch me." He gave her a hard kiss without touching her anywhere but on the mouth.

She walked them to the door. "Thank you," she whispered to Connor. "You and Jarod saved my life."

Connor kissed her cheek. "Any time, ma'am."

After they left, she closed the door and turned to Zane with such a heavy heart, she didn't know where to begin.

"There's something I have to tell you."

His mouth tightened. "Did Ned do something you didn't want Jarod to know about?"

"No. I told him everything. But while Ned had me cornered, he blurted that someone else's bid for the ranch came in higher than his." His ludicrous assumption that Jarod was the one who'd bought it revealed Ned's sickness.

Zane jumped to his feet. "Then that means we've lost the ranch."

"I'm afraid so. It's clear the bad news sent Ned's rage over the top, so he came after me." She could see the pain in Zane's eyes. "I know Jarod promised we'd get the ranch, but he's not in control of everything, so I have an idea. After we hear from Mr. Bree in the morning and know the fate of the Hensons, we'll go find us another place."

He shook his dark brown head. "You're getting married. You and Ryan will be living with Jarod. *I'll* find me a piece of property."

"I want to help. Bring your laptop into the kitchen. Let's start looking."

"Not tonight."

"Yes, tonight! It's not time for bed. We have nothing else to do. I'm anxious to see what's for sale around here. Tomorrow we'll make appointments and go check the places out with Ryan. When Jarod comes back, we'll ask him if he knows of an opportunity for us."

She thought a moment. "Keep in mind it could be a month, maybe longer, before the owner wants to move in. That'll give us time to get resettled. If the Hensons no longer have a job, we'll take them with us."

He frowned. "What do you mean *us?* When Jarod gets back, you'll be making plans for your wedding."

"I'm not doing anything until I know there's a satisfactory solution for all of us."

After a meal and a shower, Jarod took off for Sadie's ranch. With the threat of Ned gone for good, he had news for her and Zane they needed to hear. It couldn't wait until tomorrow.

Once he'd parked the truck, he hurried to the front porch and rapped on the door, thankful the last obstacle to their happiness had been removed and they could start planning their wedding.

The second Sadie opened the door, he pulled her into his arms. "I got here as fast as I could," he whispered against her mouth before devouring it. Her response was everything he could have asked for, but he sensed something was wrong. When he finally lifted his head, he saw a sadness in her eyes that had turned them a darker blue. He intended to remedy that situation right now.

"Where's Zane?"

"In the kitchen."

He brushed his mouth against hers once more. "Lead me to him. I've got news for both of you."

Her eyes misted over. "We already know what it is," she said in a quiet voice.

Surprised, Jarod shook his head. "You couldn't possibly know what I'm about to tell you."

"Ned told me while we were in the barn."

He frowned. "Told you what?"

"That Bree phoned him this afternoon and notified him an unknown buyer had purchased the ranch."

"So that *was* the final blow that sent my cousin on the rampage."

"I'm sure of it."

"Come on." He grasped her hand and walked her through to the kitchen. Zane looked up from the table where he'd set his laptop. Jarod saw the same sadness in his eyes. "Before another minute passes, I have an announcement to make."

Sadie clung to the back of one of the kitchen chairs. He could tell she was fighting not to break down. Jarod had seen that look too many times in their lives. He planned to wipe it away for good.

"The ranch and everything else on the property is yours, Zane."

Sadie looked as if she was going to faint. "Ned said you were the buyer, but I didn't believe him."

A dazed Zane got to his feet. "What's all this about?"

"We're not the buyers, and we aren't out any money. But Ralph and I didn't want Ned to get the ranch, so our attorney acted as the straw buyer to make certain you were able to purchase it before he did. Your offer was accepted, Zane."

"Jarod—" The emotion in that one word caught at his heart.

"Bree will be calling to set up a time for you to drive to Billings and sign everything. He'll give you the deed, and that will be it."

Zane cleared his throat. "I don't know what to say. 'Thank you' could never cover it." He walked over and gave him a long hug.

Jarod was moved by the other man's gratitude. "I'm the one who's in your debt. No amount of money could compensate for what you've done to help take care of Sadie and Ryan. We should have been married eight years ago, but that was not our path until now." He darted Sadie a speaking glance. "There's nothing else to prevent us from planning our future."

Zane's eyes had gone suspiciously bright. "I'm going to leave you two alone to get started on those plans."

"Did you hear all that?" Jarod whispered after Zane disappeared. Sadie was still clinging to the chair. He'd been waiting for her to run to him, but she hadn't moved. He reached for her. "What's wrong?"

Tears welled in her eyes. "How do you thank someone who's just given you the world? Tell me how you do that." Her voice shook. "I love you so desperately, Jarod, you just don't know. That's why I'm so worried to tell you something that has to be said before we talk about the wedding."

"What's happened?" He sounded anxious.

She put her hands on his chest. "This is about the children you want to have with me."

He saw fear in her eyes. "Go on."

"There's no easy way to say this. I have a heart condition you need to know about."

His own heart almost failed him. "Since when?"

"At my last rodeo two weeks before graduation, I developed palpitations. My heartbeat accelerated abnormally during the barrel racing. Mac drove me to White Lodge to see the general practitioner at the hospital. He put me on birth control and a medication that really helped, but I had to stop the barrel racing. Then he advised me to see a cardiac specialist in Billings."

"*That* was the reason I couldn't find you after your performance that night?"

She nodded. Jarod was dumbfounded. "Since we were making plans to get married and I felt all right on the medicine, I decided not to tell you about it until after we were married. But three days later you had your accident."

"Sadie—" Fear caused him to break out in a cold sweat. He gripped her shoulders. "Your mother died of a bad heart having Ryan."

"That's true, but in her case there were extenuating circumstances."

He couldn't throw this off. "How serious is your condition?"

"Don't worry. It's not fatal. As you can see I'm still alive and have been doing just fine on the medication."

"You haven't answered my question. What's wrong with you exactly?"

"Once I arrived in California and told Mother what had happened, she took me to see her heart specialist. I was diagnosed with paroxysmal supraventricular tachycardia."

"Explain that to me."

"It's called PSVT and occurs when any structure above the ventrical produces a regular, rapid electrical impulse resulting in a rapid heartbeat. The technique to fix it has been perfected and involves placing small probes in the heart that can destroy tissue and then are removed once the tissue is altered.

"The procedure is called catheter ablation. The doctor inserts a tube into a blood vessel and it's guided to your heart. A special machine sends energy through the tube. It finds and destroys small areas of heart tissue where abnormal heart rhythms may start. You have to go to the hospital to have it done."

"Did your mother undergo this procedure?"

"Yes, but it didn't work. Sadly, in her case, the arrhythmia brought on cardiac arrest, something very rare. Her older age and stress played a big factor in what happened to her. I'm thinking of having the procedure done before we're married. Otherwise I won't be getting pregnant because the medicine I take can cause a miscarriage. I'll have to stay on birth control and won't be able to give you a baby."

"I don't like it, Sadie. I don't want you to do anything that will put your life in more jeopardy than it already is."

"I'm not in jeopardy. Listen to me, Jarod. Today I talked to my heart doctor in California. He gave me the name of a specialist in Billings named Dr. Harvey who does this kind of procedure. I'm going to call tomorrow for an appointment. We'll go together. If I find out I'm a good candidate, I'd like to have it done right away."

He struggled for breath. "What if it isn't successful?"

"Then my other doctor told me they'd put in a pacemaker. But think how wonderful it would be if I could plan to get pregnant without the fear of something going wrong."

"I'd rather we adopted children."

"If it comes to that, then I'll get my tubes tied and we'll go in that direction. But more than anything in the world I want to try the procedure so I can have your baby and give it a good Crow name."

Jarod wrapped his arms all the way around her and buried his face in her hair. "More than anything in the world, the only thing I want is for you to be in my bed for the rest our lives. We have Ryan. Let's let that be enough for now. Later on we'll consider adoption."

"Will you at least be willing to go to the doctor with me?"

His eyes closed tightly. "You're asking too much. We almost lost each other before. I can't go through that again."

She eased herself away from him. "Do you really mean that?"

"I do. My mother died after she had me. Your mother died after Ryan was born. Now you're asking me to live through more torture while you undergo some procedure that could go wrong and you'd need a pacemaker to keep you alive?"

Her face was a study in pain, but he couldn't stop.

"What if that fails? Then it would mean another procedure and another until…" He shuddered. "I can't go along with it."

Sadie's complexion lost color. "What if I told you I've always wanted to have your baby and will do anything to make it possible?"

"Even chance death?"

"That won't happen! I want to do this for us. Remember what you told me a few nights ago? You said, *'The dreams I've dreamed, Sadie. My grandfather's health has to hold out long enough to see our first baby come into the world. I can hardly wait to feel movement inside you.'*"

He searched her eyes, gutted by this conversation. "I said that before I knew about your heart problem. Don't put me in this position, Sadie."

She looked at him with a pained expression. "I won't, because I can see your mind is made up." Her chin lifted in that unique way of hers. "You deserve to have your own baby. You'll make the most wonderful father on earth. So I'm going to do you a favor and release you from your commitment to me."

He stared at her, incredulous she would go this far.

"I shouldn't have accepted your proposal without telling you of my condition, but the night we got back together I wasn't thinking about babies. I was very selfish, only thinking about myself and my happiness. But let's be frank. There are many women out there like

Leslie Weston who'd give anything to meet a man like you, and they don't have my heart ailment.

"I've always been a problem for you and it hasn't stopped. One day when you have a wife and several children of your own, you'll thank me. I love you, Jarod. I'll love you till my dying breath, but you shouldn't have to sacrifice every part of your life because of me. You did enough of that while my father was alive and it simply isn't fair to you. It's your turn to find happiness."

"You really want us to be over?"

"No. I want us to have our own baby, and the only way we can do that is for me to go to the doctor to see if he can do that procedure on me. If you're too afraid to even accompany me to the appointment to find out my options, then we shouldn't be together because I don't want to put you through that kind of agony. I'm a liability and have always been."

An overwhelming sadness filled her eyes, but Jarod knew she was determined.

"I—I think you should go," she said. "After fighting a fire and subduing Ned, you must be feeling worse than exhausted."

This just couldn't be happening, but it was....

With the blackness descending upon him, Jarod left the kitchen and headed for his truck.

"Sadie Corkin, you've just done the only terrible thing in your whole life."

Shocked at the tone of Zane's voice, she wheeled around white-faced.

"Because your voices carried, I didn't have to eavesdrop. Don't let him go like this or you'll never get him back. You're the woman he's always wanted, but you just threw everything he ever did for you back in his face. Sadie... You don't tell a man it's either my way or nothing. Not a man like Jarod. You're talking about your lives here!

"The poor man hasn't had two seconds to digest all this new information. He's terrified you might die. Forget having a baby right now. Even if you didn't have a heart problem, how do you know you can get pregnant? And Jarod might not be able to give you children. You're only twenty-six. You've got years to worry about that. Jarod wants marriage. He wants to live with you. You've put having a baby before *him!*"

Sadie had never seen Zane so impassioned.

"If your positions were reversed," he went on, "and he'd given you an either/or proposition, I can guarantee you'd be in such horrendous pain I don't even want to think about it. Take my car. It's all gassed up. Go find him!"

Sadie half expected him to point a finger at her. "I don't want to see you walk in that door again without him. Remember, it's my house now. Your place is with your fiancé."

Zane was right. He was right about everything.

She dashed to the bedroom for her purse. He met her at the door with the keys. "Go get him, Sadie. All the man wants is to be loved."

"Thank you," she whispered against his cheek.

Sadie flew to the car with her purse and drove off.

Jarod usually went to the reservation when he was in pain. She knew that about him, but he'd only had a five-minute start. Just to make sure, she drove to the Bannock Ranch to check if he'd stopped there first.

Thank heaven she'd followed her instincts. There was his truck parked in front. She got out of the car and ran to the front door. Afraid to waken Ralph if he was already sleep, she knocked several times instead of using the bell. In a minute Avery opened the door.

"Sadie—"

"Hi," she said, out of breath. "Is Jarod here?"

"Yes. He passed me on the stairs a few minutes ago looking like death. You look the same way."

"I have to talk to him."

"Come on in and go up the stairs. His bedroom is at the end of the hall on the left. I'm glad you've come because you're the only one who can fix what's wrong with him."

Sadie rushed past her and raced up the steps straight into Connor, who steadied her with his hands. Her head flew back as she looked up at him. "I'm sorry, Connor. I didn't see you."

"Jarod had the same problem when he came up a few minutes ago." He grinned. "That's twice I've been run into tonight. Jarod's at the end of the hall on the left."

She nodded. "Avery told me."

"Then don't let me keep you. One piece of advice. Don't knock. Just walk in."

That wisdom from Jarod's brother told her everything. If she knocked and Jarod knew who it was, he'd tell her to go away and never come back.

Taking his advice, she hurried down the hall and started to reach for the handle when the door opened. Jarod appeared, carrying a saddlebag and bedroll. If she hadn't caught up to him in time, he'd be off to the mountains and she would never have found him.

Without hesitation, she threw her arms around his neck and clung to him, forcing him to drop his things. "I'm sorry, darling." She covered his face with kisses. "Forgive me. The second the words came out of my mouth earlier, I wished I hadn't said them."

His body remained rigid. She knew she was in for the fight of her life.

"I want to live with you. You're all I want! We'll worry about children later. I wanted everything to be perfect for us, but as Zane let me know in no uncertain terms, nothing is perfect or set in this life. We need to seize our happiness while we can. There's no life without you. Please say you forgive me."

His grave countenance made him look older. "Only on one condition. That we leave for the reservation and ask Uncle Charlo to marry us tonight."

"Tonight? Isn't it too late?"

"No. I refuse to spend another night alone without you. It's your decision."

Sadie didn't have to think. "My place is with you."

Jarod's black gaze pierced through to her soul before he shut the door behind them. "Did you drive the truck over?"

"No. Zane's car."

"Give me his keys." She followed him to Connor's room. When he appeared with Avery, Jarod said, "We're getting married tonight." He handed him the keys. "Will you two see that Zane's car is returned to him? Tell him we'll be back tomorrow."

"Sure. Can you get a marriage license this late?"

"We'll take care of that later. We don't need one on the reservation."

"In that case, I claim my right to kiss the bride ahead of time." Connor pressed a warm kiss to her lips. "Take care of my big brother," he whispered. "He badly needs to be loved by a woman like you."

Sadie nodded and threw her arms around him. "I love you, Connor."

"Welcome to the family."

"Amen," Avery chimed in from behind them and reached for Sadie. "Grandfather and I have said every known prayer in the universe for this night to happen."

She laughed through the tears. "I love both of you, too, Avery."

They walked her and Jarod out to his truck.

As they drove away, Sadie waved until she couldn't see them any longer. After closing the window, she realized Jarod was on the phone talking to his uncle. Their conversation lasted a while before he rang off.

"I want you near me." He pulled her against him so possessively, it sent a tremor through her body that didn't stop, even after they reached the reservation.

Chapter 11

The Apsáalooke settlement of two thousand looked like a surreal painting in the moonlight. Most every home had a white tepee in its yard.

Though all the signs of modern civilization were there, in her mind's eye Sadie could see the proud, courageous warriors of years ago mounted on horseback in their search for buffalo. In a fanciful moment, she could imagine Jarod riding with them, his long black hair flying in the wind.

His mother came from this wonderful heritage. Tonight Sadie was going to experience a part of it. When they pulled up in front of his uncle's house, she was excited for what was about to happen.

Pauline Black Eagle was a lovely woman who came outside with her pretty eighteen-year-old daughter Mary Black Eagle and younger son George, otherwise known as Runs Over Mountains. They were all smiling as they greeted Sadie and Jarod.

His uncle stood on the porch steps in his plaid shirt, jeans and cowboy boots. *"Kahe,"* he called to them. Jarod responded and they spoke in Siouan, the language Sadie was determined to learn.

"My uncle just welcomed us. Let's go in."

They entered the house. Once inside the living room Charlo asked them to sit. Only in his fifties, the tribal elder had obtained a *Juris* doctorate from the University of Montana School of Law. He stood in front of them, an attractive male figure with black hair to his shoulders. His dark eyes fastened on Sadie.

"My nephew says he wishes to get married. Is that your wish?"

"Yes."

"I see you wear the bracelet of our clan."

She nodded. "Jarod gave it to me eight years ago."

His eyes glimmered with satisfaction. "I once told Sits in the Center that the wolf must decide it is better to risk death for some chance of finding a mate and a territory than to live safely alone. I am happy to see he took my advice…for a second time," he added, causing her to glance at Jarod, who stared at her with smoldering eyes.

"I'm sorry about the first time and all the preparations you made that had to be canceled," Sadie said.

"It was no trouble. We were sad that Jarod had to suffer from an accident. But tonight there is only happiness because the circle of your lives has brought you together again."

"I'm so happy I could burst."

The women smiled broadly.

"My nephew has told me of your great interest in our culture, so he wishes to recreate his father and mother's wedding night. Pauline has some things for you to wear. If you'll go with her and Mary, George and I will see to Jarod and meet you outside in back. We've invited a few aunts and uncles to celebrate with you."

Jarod squeezed her hand hard before she followed the women through the house to one of the bedrooms. Sadie saw an outfit laid out on the bed.

"When my husband heard you were back from California, our clan made this deerskin dress and moccasins for you."

"But how did you know? I mean— Jarod and I hadn't been together for eight years."

"My husband sees many things."

Sadie shivered. She would always hold him in awe.

Pauline handed her the dress and Sadie looked at it with reverence. "The beading is exquisite. I'll always treasure it. Thank you from the bottom of my heart."

"You're welcome."

"You can change in my bathroom," Mary told her.

Sadie quickly removed her jeans and sweater, and emerged from the bathroom wearing the soft garment and moccasins. While she'd been changing, the other women had also donned deerskin dresses.

Pauline slipped the belt that matched the bracelet around Sadie's waist. *Bless you, Millie,* Sadie thought.

"You will please Jarod very much."

"I'll do everything I can to keep him happy."

"You already have or he wouldn't have asked you to marry him two times. Many of the women who are not married have given him a new name—*He Who Has No Eyes*. But they didn't know what my husband and I knew."

Sadie felt heat rush to her cheeks. Pauline was wonderful. She used her skills as a nurse at the tribal clinic.

Mary, who was attending college, handed Sadie the beaded earrings, which she put on. Though Sadie knew that with her blond hair she looked a fraud, it was exciting to play a role for a little while. The most important role of her life. *Jarod's bride.*

"Come with us."

She walked with them through the house and out the back door to the yard. A fire had been lit in the fire pit, casting shadows over the tall white tepee in the background. The magical setting sent goose bumps up and down Sadie's arms.

Several dozen extended family members stood in a semicircle. She marveled that Charlo could assemble so many of their loved ones this close to midnight. They nodded to Sadie, who stayed close to Pauline and Mary. Their presence showed how much they revered Jarod.

Another minute and Charlo came out the back door in deerskin pants and shirt, followed by George in a similar outfit. Jarod walked out last. To her surprise he was wearing modern-day jeans and cowboy boots. But he'd dressed in a black ribbon shirt with a V neck and long sleeves ending in cuffs the men wore for special occasions.

She knew black was the sacred color of the Apsáalooke. The ribbons reflected orange, green, blue and yellow, representing the elements. The intricate pattern would have been passed down through the generations and given to him by his uncle.

Jarod had never worn his hair in a braid before, at least not in front of her. She could hardly breathe, he looked so fiercely handsome. Suddenly his gaze fell on her. Time stood still as they communed in silence as she took in the gravity of this moment. A light breeze ruffled the tips of her hair. If there was any sound, it was the thud of her heart in the soft night air.

Charlo motioned for her and Jarod to come closer and face him. A hush fell as he began to speak.

"If Chief Plenty Coups were here, he would say the ground on which we stand is sacred ground. It is the dust and blood of our ancestors. Sadie... Tonight when you enter the tepee on this sacred ground, our First Maker reminds you to remember that a woman's highest calling is to lead a man's soul so as to unite him with his Source."

She wasn't sure how to respond but gave him a solemn nod.

"Jarod? Tonight when you enter the tepee on this sacred ground, our First Maker would have you remember that a man's highest calling is to protect a woman so she is free to walk the earth unharmed."

When he nodded, Sadie wanted to proclaim to everyone that he'd always protected her and had already saved her from Ned earlier in the day.

"The crow reveals the true path to life's mission. It merges both light and dark, inner and outer, and when in the darkness of emotional pain and turmoil, the crow will carry the lost soul into the light.

"Both of you have endured much sorrow over the years. Don't waste today letting too much of yesterday ruin your joy. Before you lie down together, give thanks for blessings already on their way and you will have peace."

What better advice could anyone give?

He lifted his hands. "Go now. May you live in eternal happiness."

They were married?

She asked the question with her eyes. Jarod's mouth broke into such a beautiful smile that her entire being was filled with indescribable love for him. He grasped her hand. Leading her around the fire to the tepee, he moved the buffalo covering aside so she could enter.

The tepee's cone shape was formed with dozens of poles and could hold five to six people. Blankets on top of buffalo skins had been placed on the floor. Nothing else was inside....

Jarod held both her hands. "My mother's culture didn't do marriage ceremonies, but I think my uncle did the perfect job of performing ours."

"So do I," she said softly. There was enough light from the fire outside to see each other.

"Do you mind if we kneel right now and do what he said?"

He kissed both her hands before they got down on their knees, facing each other. "You say the prayer."

"Thank you. I want to."

Closing her eyes she said, "Dear God, my heart is full to overflowing for the many blessings Thou has given us. We will strive to live worthily of the blessings Thou has yet to bestow on us. I thank Thee for my husband, a great man and a great warrior. I thank Thee for Jarod's loving family both on the ranch and on the reservation. I thank Thee for my family, for the Hensons. Amen."

Jarod's eyes were fastened on her as she lifted her head. "Amen," he whispered in a husky voice. "You have no idea how beautiful you are to me, kneeling there in that dress to please me. Though I see a woman, I also see the sweet, vulnerable, lonely girl inside you who stole my heart years ago. I want to fill your loneliness, Sadie."

She cradled his face with her hands. "You already have. Uncle Charlo said not to dwell on the past. Tonight is the beginning of our future. There's something I want to do before we do anything else."

His breathing grew shallow. "What is it?"

"Take off your shirt first."

He looked surprised, but he did as she asked. Her breath caught to see his well-defined chest and shoulders emerge. "Now close your eyes."

As soon as they were closed, she moved around behind him and began unbraiding his fabulous hair. "I've been dying to do this since you came up to me at the funeral." She threaded her fingers through the glossy strands that fell loose and swung around his shoulders and face.

When she was finished she knelt in front of him. "You can open them now." Sadie almost fell back in amazement. "You're the most gorgeous man. I want an oil painting done of you exactly like this, sitting inside this tepee. After it's framed, I'll hang it in the most prominent place in our home with a small brass plate at the bottom that reads 'He Who Sits At My Side.'"

Jarod's eyes glowed like black fire. He rose to his full height. She noticed the special belt he wore before he pulled her up and turned her around. Her body trembled as he undid the back of her dress, lowering it off her shoulders till it fell to her feet. His mouth found the side of her neck. "Come lie with me, my love."

A cry of longing escaped her lips as he laid her gently on top of the blankets. Looking down at her he said, "No painting of you could do you justice. I love you, Sadie. You're my heart's blood."

After plunging his fingers through her silky hair, he lowered his mouth to hers, giving her the husband's kiss she'd been waiting for since she'd fallen in love with him at fifteen.

Jarod— As their bodies melded, her heart and soul leaped to meet his.

Morning had come to the reservation. Jarod could see light through the tiny opening at the top of the tepee. He eased himself away from his precious wife, who still slept.

Jarod's hunger for her hadn't been appeased, no matter how many times they'd made love during the night. Now that he'd finally allowed her to sleep, he left her tangled in the blanket while he peered outside the entrance. The direction of the sun shining overhead told him it was at least two o'clock in the afternoon. That's why the interior was heating up.

He caught sight of their regular clothes along with a picnic basket of food Pauline had placed against the outside of the tepee. She'd taken care of everything to make their wedding night perfect.

After struggling eight years along a treacherous path, he'd obtained his heart's desire. Sadie was the most unselfish, giving woman he'd ever known.

Jarod breathed in the fresh air, aware that he felt whole at last. The night had been so perfect, he never wanted it to end, but she would awaken soon and want to get back to Ryan. Recognizing his insatiable appetite for her, he decided he'd better get dressed or they'd be here for another twelve hours.

Once he'd pulled on his cowboy boots, he brought everything inside. He found his cell phone and watch among his clothes and checked for messages. Only one from Connor.

Grandfather is ecstatic and can't wait to welcome both of you home. Tyson and Ned's par-

ents are inconsolable. The police need to know
if you want to press charges. You have every
right, bro.

"Darling?" He glanced over at his wife. The
word still thrilled him. What a beautiful sight
she made. Unable to resist, he leaned down
to kiss her, which was a mistake. He wanted
to climb under the covers with her and never
come out.

"Why did you let me sleep?"

"Because you needed to after I wore you
out." He put the basket in front of them. "Pauline fixed us a picnic."

"She's incredible."

"I agree."

"I saw you checking your messages just
now. Anything from Zane about Ryan?"

"No. It was from Connor. Everything's fine.
Let's enjoy our first meal together as man
and wife."

They ate sandwiches and drank soda. "I'm
so excited to be married to you, I can hardly
take it in. Last night—"

"Was miraculous," he broke in. "No man
ever had a lover like you."

Her blush delighted him. When he'd finished eating, he reached for his thong.

"Don't confine your hair. I love the way it flows."

"I'll wear it loose at night, but during the day it gets in the way."

She eyed him curiously. "Yesterday you were going to tell me why you changed your hair."

He swallowed the rest of his cola. "I paid a trip to the beauty salon in White Lodge to talk to a woman named Rosie."

In another minute she knew the whole story about Ned's fabrication.

"She washed and cut your hair!"

"What's wrong?"

"I want you to know that no other woman will ever be allowed to do that again."

Laughter poured out of Jarod. He pressed her back against the blankets, kissing her long and hard.

"I want your promise, Jarod."

"I swear I'll never go in there again."

"Rosie probably had a cow when she found out she was going to get her hands on the gorgeous Jarod Bannock."

"A cow?" he teased.

"You know what I mean. I bet she can't wait until you go back."

He couldn't stop laughing. "She's married."

"That doesn't matter. For years I've had to put up with the way women look at you. It's been enough to give me a heart attack."

"Don't say that," he begged her, "not even in jest."

"Sorry. Happily, Pauline told me something about you that makes me feel a lot better."

"What's that?"

"The women on the reservation have been calling you He Who Has No Eyes."

More laughter caused him to bury his face in her throat. "That's because only one woman has ever held my heart."

"Have I told you I'm madly in love with you?"

"All night long," he murmured against her lips.

"Darling? What was Connor's message? I know it had to be something important or he wouldn't have sent it."

"Tell you what." He reached for her regular clothes and handed them to her. "After you get dressed, we'll freshen up in the house and then I'll tell you during the drive home.

On the way we'll stop in White Lodge for our marriage license."

She smiled. "It's a little late for that, wouldn't you say?"

He didn't say anything, but fell back against the blankets to watch her.

"Close your eyes."

"That's one thing I can't do."

"The trouble with this tepee is that there's nothing to hide behind."

"My Apsáalooke ancestors knew what they were doing," he teased.

"Your *male* ancestors."

He loved it that she tried her hardest to pretend he wasn't there while she put on her clothes. Sadie never did seem to know how beautiful she was. Everything about her made her so desirable to him, and he was terrified of ever losing her. Their argument over her wanting that heart procedure still had a stranglehold on him.

Her blue eyes flashed. "I'm ready now, as if you didn't know."

"You did that far too fast for my liking. Next time things will be different."

"*How* different?"

"For one thing, we won't be in a hurry to

go anywhere." His comment put color in her cheeks.

He gathered up their things and they left the tepee. No one was home when they went inside to use the bathroom. Jarod wrote a note and left it on the counter, thanking his aunt and uncle for everything.

We're now one soul in two bodies and have come into the light.

As they drove away from the reservation toward home, Sadie nestled up against him and pressed kisses to his jaw. "Tell me about Connor's message."

"Ned is in huge trouble. But I don't want to talk about him right now."

Sadie looped her arms around his neck. "You're such a noble man, Jarod Bannock." She started kissing him until he could hardly see to drive. "Sorry," she whispered when he had to slow down. "I'll behave myself until we get home."

"That's the next thing I want to talk to you about, *Mrs. Bannock.* I'm planning to build us our own home on the ranch, but until we've decided what kind we want and how big to make it, where is our home going to be for the next few months?"

"Would you mind terribly moving in with me? The nursery's already set up for Ryan, and it's only a few minutes away from your ranch and Ralph."

"Sadie, I'd live anywhere with you and can bring over some of my clothes. In fact, it's the Apsáalooke way for the husband to move in with the wife's family. But you'll need to feel Zane out."

"Honestly, I know he won't care. He's been looking for work."

"What about his plan to become a rancher?"

"With Mac's help, I think he wants to try to do both." For the rest of the drive home, she told him about Zane's interest in working for the BLM as a ranger.

When they arrived at the ranch, Jarod pulled up next to the Volvo. Sadie jumped out and they both hurried in the house.

"Zane?"

"In the kitchen, Sadie."

They found him alone. "Where's Ryan?"

He got up from the table where he'd been working on the laptop. "Millie and Liz wanted to watch him at their house. They're keeping him overnight so you can have some alone time."

"You're kidding—"

His eyes zeroed in on Jarod. "That's an amazing shirt you're wearing."

"It's a ribbon shirt with a design from his clan woven into the strips appliquéd to the fabric. Isn't it beautiful? Jarod wore it for the wedding ceremony."

"Nice." Zane's brows lifted. "What did *you* wear?"

"A beautiful, beaded deerskin dress. It's out in the truck. I'll show it to you."

"What are you doing home already? You're supposed to be on your honeymoon. I hoped you'd enjoy another night on the reservation at least!"

"We couldn't have done that to you. When I left here last night, I didn't even know if Jarod would forgive me. I caught him leaving the bedroom with his bedroll."

He grinned. "Yeah?" His gaze flicked to Jarod. "How long did it take you to decide to get married instead of high-tailing it to the mountains?"

"Not long," Jarod admitted.

"Well, now that you're here, I might as

well tell you about the conversation I had with Connor and Avery last night when they brought back my car."

Jarod was all ears.

"They said they didn't know your plans yet, but figured if you two wanted to live here with Ryan for the next few weeks while you figure everything out, it could be like a honeymoon for you. Because of your grandfather, they know you wouldn't want to go away yet.

"In the meantime I'll temporarily move into your room, Jarod. It's only an idea, but let's be honest… You two need some space, and you won't get it at *your* ranch. We'll all split up the babysitting."

"It's a fabulous idea!" Sadie cried.

Jarod could see Connor coming up with that idea, but *his sister?* Avery was such a private person.

"My room's yours, Zane. I'm building Sadie and me a new house, so I don't plan to be in it any longer."

"In that case, why don't you two go see your grandfather? I understand he can't wait to congratulate you. When you come back, I'll drive over with a few of my things."

Sadie hugged Zane before they went back out to the truck.

"Before we leave, I want another one of these." Jarod gave her a kiss that she returned with such passion, he couldn't wait for night to come.

When he would have let her go, she clung to him. "I think I'm in shock. For almost thirty years this ranch was off-limits to you. Now we're going to live here and we're married, and Zane and Ryan are happy and it's all because of you and—" She couldn't finish what she was trying to say.

Jarod knew she was happy, but not completely. The next step on their path would be the decision about children. When he'd awakened this morning with her lying in his arms, he'd remembered something he'd been taught by his father about fear when they were trying to tame a horse out in the corral. It had been speaking to him all day.

Courage was not the absence of fear, but rather the judgment that something else was more important than fear. Sadie wanted his baby. He wanted to give her his baby. To do that, he had to overcome his fear.

Tonight they'd talk about his going to the doctor with her.

He drove them to the ranch. Ralph was waiting for them in the living room with Jarod's siblings. They'd thrown together a quick celebratory meal with champagne. For the next hour they sat around and talked about the ceremony and the outpouring of love from Charlo's family.

"Thank you for doing this for us. To be here with all of you in the home I've known all of my life, and to be with my wife, whom I've loved for so long, I—" Jarod couldn't go on. His heart was too full.

In his whole life he'd never known such a completeness of joy, but he couldn't forget Connor's text message. There was something important they needed to discuss.

"What's happened to Ned?"

Ralph cleared his throat. "He and Owen have both been taken into custody and will be arraigned before the judge. Naturally his parents are grieving. I told the police you were on your honeymoon. They want to speak to you when you get back and are waiting for you to press charges for the accident."

Jarod clasped Sadie around the shoulders

before letting out a deep sigh. "Marrying Sadie has made me so happy, any feelings of revenge I've wrestled with have fled. In their place is a deep sadness."

Sadie nodded. "At this point that's how I feel about my father, too."

He stared at his family. "Ned has been sick for years, but I don't believe he's evil. Perhaps there's still time for him to heal if he gets the kind of intense therapy and counseling he needs. Tomorrow I'll have a talk with Grant. Even if it takes years, I'd rather see Ned go that route than face a felony charge. As for Owen, he was only doing what Ned wanted, but Owen wasn't the one who drove into me. I'd say he needs therapy, too."

"You're a fine man, Jarod," his grandfather told him, trying to hold back the tears. "You make us all proud."

"To finally have peace so we can get on with our lives means the world to us, doesn't it, sweetheart?"

Sadie kissed his cheek. "Jarod and I have loved each other for what has seemed like eternity. It's hard to believe we can actually plan for the future."

"We want a family, but first Sadie has to

undergo an operation on her heart to fix the palpitations. I just found out it's the reason she stopped barrel racing."

Sadie's look of joy and gratitude made him realize it was the right decision.

"Once that's behind us, then we'll start to build our own home on the property. With Zane next door to help us raise Ryan, life couldn't get any better. Speaking of Zane, we need to get back to the ranch so he can start to move in here." Jarod got to his feet, pulling Sadie with him.

Sadie moved around the room to hug everyone. "We were given wonderful advice by Jarod's uncle. He said, 'Both of you have endured much sorrow over the years. Don't waste today letting too much of yesterday ruin your joy. Before you lie down together, give thanks for blessings already on their way and you will have peace.'

"Jarod and I are going to take his advice and remember it. We love all of you."

Jarod's throat tightened.

He was going home with his angelic wife. Today was their first step to a shared destiny.

* * * * *

HOME on the RANCH

Get 4 FREE REWARDS!

We'll send you 2 FREE Books plus 2 FREE Mystery Gifts.

Harlequin® Special Edition books feature heroines finding the balance between their work life and personal life on the way to finding true love.

FREE
Value Over
$20

Get 4 FREE REWARDS!

We'll send you 2 FREE Books plus 2 FREE Mystery Gifts.

FREE
Value Over
$20

Both the **Romance** and **Suspense** collections feature compelling novels written by many of today's best-selling authors.

YES! Please send me 2 FREE novels from the Essential Romance or Essential Suspense Collection and my 2 FREE gifts (gifts are worth about $10 retail). After receiving them, if I don't wish to receive any more books, I can return the shipping statement marked "cancel." If I don't cancel, I will receive 4 brand-new novels every month and be billed just $6.74 each in the U.S. or $7.24 each in Canada. That's a savings of at least 16% off the cover price. It's quite a bargain! Shipping and handling is just 50¢ per book in the U.S. and 75¢ per book in Canada*. I understand that accepting the 2 free books and gifts places me under no obligation to buy anything. I can always return a shipment and cancel at any time. The free books and gifts are mine to keep no matter what I decide.

Choose one: ☐ **Essential Romance**   ☐ **Essential Suspense**
                (194/394 MDN GMY7)   (191/391 MDN GMY7)

Name (please print)

Address   Apt. #

City   State/Province   Zip/Postal Code

Mail to the **Reader Service:**
IN U.S.A.: P.O. Box 1341, Buffalo, NY 14240-8531
IN CANADA: P.O. Box 603, Fort Erie, Ontario L2A 5X3

Want to try two free books from another series! Call 1-800-873-8635 or visit www.ReaderService.com.

---

*Terms and prices subject to change without notice. Prices do not include applicable taxes. Sales tax applicable in NY. Canadian residents will be charged applicable taxes. Offer not valid in Quebec. This offer is limited to one order per household. Books received may not be as shown. Not valid for current subscribers to the Essential Romance or Essential Suspense Collection. All orders subject to approval. Credit or debit balances in a customer's account(s) may be offset by any other outstanding balance owed by or to the customer. Please allow 4 to 6 weeks for delivery. Offer available while quantities last.

Your Privacy—The Reader Service is committed to protecting your privacy. Our Privacy Policy is available online at www.ReaderService.com or upon request from the Reader Service. We make a portion of our mailing list available to reputable third parties that offer products we believe may interest you. If you prefer that we not exchange your name with third parties, or if you wish to clarify or modify your communication preferences, please visit us at www.ReaderService.com/consumerschoice or write to us at Reader Service Preference Service, P.O. Box 9062, Buffalo, NY 14240-9062. Include your complete name and address.

STRS18

Get 4 FREE REWARDS!

We'll send you 2 FREE Books plus 2 FREE Mystery Gifts.

Harlequin® Heartwarming™ Larger-Print books feature traditional values of home, family, community and most of all—love.

FREE
Value Over
$20

YES! Please send me 2 FREE Harlequin® Heartwarming™ Larger-Print novels and my 2 FREE mystery gifts (gifts worth about $10 retail). After receiving them, if I don't wish to receive any more books, I can return the shipping statement marked "cancel." If I don't cancel, I will receive 4 brand-new larger-print novels every month and be billed just $5.49 per book in the U.S. or $6.24 per book in Canada. That's a savings of at least 19% off the cover price. It's quite a bargain! Shipping and handling is just 50¢ per book in the U.S. and 75¢ per book in Canada*. I understand that accepting the 2 free books and gifts places me under no obligation to buy anything. I can always return a shipment and cancel at any time. The free books and gifts are mine to keep no matter what I decide.

161/361 IDN GMY3

Name (please print)

Address   Apt. #

City   State/Province   Zip/Postal Code

Mail to the **Reader Service:**
IN U.S.A.: P.O. Box 1341, Buffalo, NY 14240-8531
IN CANADA: P.O. Box 603, Fort Erie, Ontario L2A 5X3

Want to try two free books from another series! Call 1-800-873-8635 or visit www.ReaderService.com.

READERSERVICE.COM

Manage your account online!

- Review your order history
- Manage your payments
- Update your address

> ### *We've designed the Reader Service website just for you.*

Enjoy all the features!

- Discover new series available to you, and read excerpts from any series.
- Respond to mailings and special monthly offers.
- Browse the Bonus Bucks catalog and online-only exculsives.
- Share your feedback.

Visit us at:

ReaderService.com